WINTER

DECEPTION

by

Sally Jo Pitts

Mystery and Suspense

Women sleuths

ISBN: 978-1-952661-23-5

WINTER DECEPTION

iii

Lay not up for yourselves treasures upon earth, where moth and rust doth corrupt, and where thieves break through and steal.

Matthew 6:19 (KJV)

Acknowledgments:

A book requires many helpers to come together.

I appreciate the critique work of Marcia Lahti, Larry Bruce, fellow Writers Aglow participants, and my frontline readers: Tommy and Jennifer Vaughan-Birch.

Thanks goes to veteran law enforcement officer Mitchell Pitts, who helped me with technical information regarding crime scene and arrest procedures and to Eric Unger and Molly May who brainstormed some critical motivation plot points.

I am grateful to Cynthia Hickey with Winged Publications who believed in this Seasons of Mystery project and created the cover design.

CHAPTER ONE

Private Investigator Robert Grey grabbed the crystal goblet that clipped the edge of gold-trimmed plate before it toppled over. His heart pounded in the same way it might have if confronted by a knife-wielding criminal. Facing bad guys in bars, nightspots or parking lots was more his speed. Fancy luncheons in an antebellum dining room with vintage family crest china, and an embossed menu card were foreign to him.

He leaned forward in the dining chair, avoiding the carved ridges of the chair back designed for looks, not comfort. At the invitation of Attorney Cameo Clark seated to his left, he and his intern Jane Carson had arrived at Topazus, the Clark family plantation in South Carolina. The imposing manor stood as a bastion of old southern charm at the end of a long drive lined with moss-laden oak trees. They were there to enjoy Christmas events while conducting research on the developer interested in buying the estate.

Robert's law enforcement background triggered

him to locate the windows, and doors in the room for entry and exit. But he also spotted the crown molding, wainscoting, and decorative ceiling medallion above the chandelier that he wouldn't have noticed it weren't for Jane.

She had supplied live audio book narration during the nine-hour drive from Mobile, Alabama. "Topazus was built for Morgan Danford Clark and his wife Martha Lee in 1842. The name of the estate is derived from the rare red topaz Morgan mined in South America and had fashioned into a ring for his wife."

Jane's love for history and research had provided him with a crash course on the story behind the plantation along with the surrounding region. No surprise that she was enthused about the trip. What did surprise him was that he enjoyed hearing the stories she shared, especially about the impact of the Civil War in the area and the use of Topazus as an infantry hospital.

Now that they had arrived, he was ready to complete his assignment for Cameo. Running backgrounds and conducting interviews, Robert could handle. What he didn't feel comfortable with was this hoity-toity luncheon and the place setting that vexed him.

According to the Topazus Carte Du Jour, assorted garden greens with roasted carrots and lemon-pepper dressing sat before him. Which fork should he use on the tangy smelling mixture? And was the monogrammed cloth napkin in the golden ring for looks or use? Sharing the table with eight other guests, he didn't want to commit a major gaffe.

Robert nudged Jane. She cocked an eyebrow and leaned toward him.

"I need a quick lesson in etiquette."

Smirking, she pulled her napkin from its holder and spread it in her lap.

He'd met Jane at the cancer support group for family members after his wife died and offered her an internship in his agency opened after his recent retirement from law enforcement. She'd been a fast learner, which he needed to be right now.

"Is it my turn to issue rules?"

"Lay it on me. Which fork do I use?"

"Work from the outside in."

"What about the three-pronged item above my plate?"

"It's for dessert."

What was wrong with using one fork for everything?

She pointed. "That is your beverage and you pass food to the right."

"How many rules are there?"

"Lots."

Robert scowled. "I don't dump investigator mandates on you all at once."

"You'll be fine. Just follow my lead."

He followed and tolerated her smug grin.

"Jane, I understand you're a private investigator. Sounds thrilling." The comment came from Rita Parsons, seated opposite Jane. Cameo had introduced Rita as a long-time family friend and caterer who was overseeing the luncheon.

"PI intern," Jane said. "I'm really a kindergarten teacher on temporary leave." Jane turned toward Cameo. "But the murder case we worked last month offered enough thrills to last me a while."

Cameo smiled and raised a thumbs up. "Robert and Jane have made quite a team. They exposed a killer and cleared my client. After working so hard, I thought spending Christmas on the plantation would give them time to relax and unwind." She left off the part about the confidential investigation she had assigned.

Attorney Alfred Berdanier, the estate trustee seated directly across from Robert, addressed him. "Cameo says you're a retired lawman. You don't look old enough to be retired."

"I started at nineteen, right out of standards training, and put in twenty-five years." He was forty-four and would have stayed in law enforcement longer, but life had thrown him a curve.

Berdanier's bushy eyebrows met in the middle. "Working for Cameo puts you on the wrong side of the system, doesn't it?"

Robert bit down hard on a salad crouton. Bullseye. The comment hit gut level. As a lawman, he cringed when defense attorneys championed criminals and sought or created loopholes to turn them loose. A crafty lawyer like Cameo could argue white is black and make you believe it. Truth: working as a private investigator for defense instead of prosecution did give him wrong-side twinges at times. He cleared his throat to respond but was too late. Cameo took over. Head of the table suited her.

"A sanctimonious Alfred Berdanier? You surprise me. You know many people accused of crimes aren't guilty. But guilty or not, my job as a defense attorney is to help my client navigate the legal system. Right, Robert?"

She made a good point. Defendants did need the

assistance of a lawyer to deal with legalities. "The way I see it, an investigator, whether private or government, should work just as hard to prove a man is innocent as he is guilty."

"Well," Rita's voice lilted with a cheery edge, "no matter the side of the law you work for, I hope you two have found your accommodations satisfactory."

Robert and Jane had been assigned rooms in the separate bed-and-breakfast building behind the mansion's gardens.

"Jane, I had an idea the red room with its Hepplewhite furnishings might suit you. The desk chair in the room was once used in the Topazus drawing room."

"A lovely room and—" Jane began.

But Rita talked over her. "I selected the green room for you, Robert. The first Morgan Clark purchased the four-poster bed in Europe. The carved cherry wood headers are magnificent."

To Robert, a bed was a bed. What he did notice was no TV. "The room is terrific, and I will be sure to take note of those headers."

Rita's nod accentuated her upswept hairdo pulled tight enough to erase wrinkles. "My pleasure to host you both."

Berdanier reached plump hands into the breadbasket and said, "I believe the hostessing title belongs to the Clark ladies at the ends of the table." He handled all the rolls and finally settled on one, slathered it with butter, and took a big bite.

Cameo grabbed the basket with a scowl which told Robert that Berdanier hadn't used proper breadbasket protocol.

"Of course," Rita tittered, "but as caterer for the bed-and-breakfast and this luncheon—"

"You needn't sugarcoat titles for me." Katherine Clark, Cameo's mother, spoke in the same authoritative manner as her daughter from the opposite end of the table. The bold slash of silver that cut across the front of her chestnut hair resembled the mark of Zorro.

"The small plate to your left is for bread and butter," Jane whispered to Robert.

Berdanier didn't need a bread plate. He devoured his roll in two bites.

"Gracious of you." Berdanier said and sent a head bow to Katherine.

"I'm not sure gracious is the right word. Sitting at the table end holds no real meaning, as you well know." She arched one eyebrow. "Besides, I have gladly relinquished the hostessing duty to Rita." Katherine acknowledged Rita with a head tilt. "Ever since we were Belles, it was obvious she was made for the role."

"Ah. A mistress minus the master," Berdanier said.

"Too bad Rita had to settle for second best." The comment came from Dean Parsons seated to Katherine's left. He had been introduced as a realtor and representative for the Chandler Company that Robert was to investigate.

"You flatter yourself with that high a ranking," Rita shot back at him.

"I shall rephrase." His stark white hair shimmered in the chandelier's light as he lifted his hand and pointed to himself. "I was the poor schmuck who married you on the rebound and thought it best for all to bounce out after a few *long* years."

The poor schmuck? Second best? Dean was Rita's

ex?

Micah, the estate's foreman, nudged Dean with the breadbasket. Dean took a roll from the basket and passed it to Katherine.

"You are entertaining." Rita snickered and lifted her chin. "At least our relationship produced James." She patted the hand of her son seated next to her. He was a thirty-something attorney with a hairline retreating on either side of a widow's peak.

Dean sipped his water and set the goblet down. Both father and son locked eyes. Dean gave a perfunctory nod. "That we did. If Katherine hadn't stolen Morgan from you, there would have been no James."

"What are Belles?" Jane asked.

Jane to the rescue. The conversation had headed south, but the banter between Robert's potential interviewees had generated questions he could ask later concerning the sale of the property.

"Belles and Beaus were my grandmother's brainchild," Cameo said. "High school students train as docents, learning the plantation's history and wearing costumes from the 1800s. Rita was in the first group of Belles."

Rita's face brightened. "I was a sophomore in high school and recruited Katherine to be a Belle when she moved here our senior year. The tradition is still in place." Rita pointed at the young woman dressed in a black uniform and white bib apron, serving them. "Mary Sue was once a Belle. With her experience, I was glad to hire her."

Jane whispered to Robert, "Place your fork across the salad plate to indicate you are finished."

He barely had time to assimilate the latest rule when Berdanier quipped.

"Interesting. It may be a Belle trait to steal masters from their missus. A fair assessment, Mary Sue?" He flipped the basket cozy aside to reveal one remaining roll and took it.

Mary Sue flushed a bright pink, grabbed the breadbasket, and disappeared through the kitchen door.

"Alfred," Cameo scolded Berdanier. "Why embarrass the girl?"

"I have my reasons." He buttered his roll with a flourish.

Rita got up, "I'd better check on her."

With the swiveling neck of a tennis spectator, Robert paused to place his fork across his salad plate and looked to Jane for approval.

She nodded.

Berdanier continued. "And I have several reasons for wanting to meet with you today, Cameo. I have prepared reports."

"What about?" Cameo asked.

"The estate's poor financial status, for one."

"Financial reports can mislead, depending on the way they are displayed." James dropped his words of wisdom, but no one acknowledged his remark.

"Financial supervision is your job." Cameo tugged a strand of thick hair like her mother's behind her ear and addressed Berdanier with knife-edged words. "Is now really the time to bring this up with guests here?"

"Guests?" Berdanier blurted. "They're your employees and I'm sure they will understand. The people gathered here all have an interest in the estate, which is supposed to be self-supporting. Micah, tell us how you intend to make the farm profitable again. It has become a liability and not an asset."

Jane started to pull a tiny notebook from her purse. Robert touched her wrist and gave a slight head shake. Reading body language was more important than writing right now.

Seated next to Jane on the same side of the table, Micah spoke in a distinctive baritone. "It's true. We've had some disastrous growing seasons. I've lost cotton crops in the Thousand-Year Flood, followed by Hurricanes Matthew and Florence. But I have two hundred acres plowed and prepared for a good crop this upcoming year."

"I'd have thought you would have learned how to plan for such problems in your agribusiness courses," Berdanier said. Micah's grip took a stranglehold on his fork while Berdanier swallowed the last of his roll and dusted his hands together. "The Topazus ring's being stolen saved the day last year. The insurance money has kept this plantation afloat."

"If it took the theft of the family's rare topaz to keep the estate viable, I question *your* management capabilities." Cameo had delicate features but a harsh back-at-you courtroom technique that zinged. She twisted a bite from her roll and popped it in her mouth. "I received a call from an environmental office inquiring about a Roger Underwood and mineral leasing. I was in the dark, but apparently, you're not?"

Berdanier's ears reddened as Cameo pressed on. "And how is it the ring conveniently disappeared? Insurance fraud is a criminal offense."

Slamming his water glass on the table, his dessert fork jumped and clinked against his plate. Berdanier said, "Are you suggesting—"

"I'm suggesting it may be time to rid the estate of the middleman," Cameo said.

Berdanier eyes narrowed and he faced Cameo. "Don't forget Sandra Cathey. There are some offenses that have no statute of limitations and a middleman was your salvation."

Cameo's face drained of color.

Attorney Berdanier, having drawn blood, launched a barb in a different direction. "As for the ring, Rita discovered it was missing. I merely reported it." He clipped words at the end of his sentences.

Rita returned from the kitchen with a steaming platter. Mary Sue, composed but solemn, removed salad plates. "Cameo, please serve yourself and pass the entrée," Rita said.

Cameo, visibly shaken, tried to accept the dish but almost dropped it. Robert reached for the serving piece and held it for her.

Rita didn't seem to notice Cameo's near slip and continued talking. "This is my signature chicken with a special cranberry orange sauce," she said with flair and returned to her seat.

"Not to brag, but I helped Mother perfect the seasoning on this dish." James leaned to one side for Mary Sue to clear his plate and clasped his hands in bravo style. "Culinary dabbling is a hobby."

"James did help me. A man that loves to cook will make a fine catch," Rita said and sent a smile in Cameo's direction.

Robert slid two chicken breasts onto his plate and breathed in the warm citrusy bouquet. The scent swirled around and mixed with his investigative juices. The questions of correct utensil use pestered him, but inquiries around mineral leasing, liabilities, and theft, drew him like a Bluetick Coonhound on a track.

Berdanier flicked at crumbs on his tie and spoke to Cameo. "The topaz ring is among the matters I wish to discuss after lunch."

Rita jerked around; a strand of hair sprung loose. "Really, must you do that today? I was counting on Cameo and James trying on their costumes after lunch, in case adjustments are needed before the Christmas events."

Robert imitated Jane's use of fork and knife as she commented. "Stepping back in time and wearing antebellum fashions sounds intriguing."

To Robert it sounded about as intriguing as a cold bath on a winter night. But Jane's being charmed by this place pleased Robert.

"I visited Topazus with my aunt when I was ten, and I'm thrilled to return. I'm surprised you don't live in this house," Jane said to Katherine.

Katherine huffed. "Stay in this damp, musty place? No, thank you. Be glad you're staying in the bed-and-breakfast rooms behind the gardens. I'm happier in my house on the hill, even though I'm harassed by squirrels and raccoons."

"Coons are intelligent creatures and clean. They like to wash their food." James inserted another unsolicited tidbit.

"I don't know about intelligent," Dean said. "I was grilling steaks last night on Katherine's patio and a coon jumped from the picnic table onto the grate, going for the steak. The crazy animal had to have burned his feet. Unbelievable. He knocked the grill over and made

11

a mess."

"The squirrels wreak havoc on my bird feeders too." Katherine squinted. "I keep my .22 rifle handy by the back door."

"You don't want to mess with Katherine. She's an expert shot." Dean said.

"Another Belle trait. My mom is a dandy shot too," James said.

Amazing. Two guys sparring over which lady was the best shot.

Micah spoke up. "Ladies, I could use your expertise on the farm. Besides the flood and hurricanes, we've had trouble with squirrels and rodents getting into the cotton seed."

"What about the flood water?" Cameo asked Berdanier. "Have you had the house checked for mold?"

"Again, another topic to address—" Berdanier began and Rita interrupted.

"I was concerned too. I had James' friend Brandon, who has a restoration business, check for mold. He gave the house a clean bill of health."

Berdanier lifted his brows. "Really? You've played mistress here so long; I believe you think you own the place."

Stabbing the chicken on her plate with a fork, Rita used her knife to saw off a bite with a vengeance. "I am here more than any of you, except Micah."

"Exactly what topics are on your list?" Cameo asked. She'd regained color and seemed back in command.

Berdanier held up an index finger. "Number one, insurance. We can't afford what they charge to insure a house that would go up like kindling if it caught fire. There is no sprinkling system or fire hydrant close by."

"Are you saying we are no longer insured?"

"We've got liability, not replacement."

"All the more reason to consider Chandler Development's purchase proposal," Dean said.

Katherine nodded. Rita glared.

"Chandler Development is on my list," Berdanier said. "And Dean is here to answer questions regarding their proposal. But selling the property means dealing with historical preservation and heirs' property."

Katherine threw her shoulders back. "What? Preservation? Heirs' property? Since when are those issues?"

Rita perked up.

"There's a new law, the Clementa Pinckney Partition of Heirs' Property Act to be exact. It could sabotage a sale." James again.

"What are you talking about?" Cameo asked.

James lifted his hand, palm outward, and offered more information. "The act pertains to descendants of slaves who live on land inherited without clear title. Micah living on Topazus is an excellent example. Early black landowners didn't make wills, largely due to a lack of access to legal resources."

Berdanier nodded. "If descendants of slaves belonging to the Clarks filed a claim, the property could be designated as heirs' property, which would sabotage and throw a monkey wrench into a property sale."

"Sabotage? Monkey wrench? You make it sound underhanded for ancestors of slaves making property claims." Micah's fists rested in tight balls beside his plate. "The original owner of this plantation freed his

13

slaves," he jabbed his chest, "my ancestors. And we've been on the land for seven generations. Bad enough you challenged my farming ability. But there has always been an understanding about property rights. I take offense at your remarks."

Micah was articulate and knowledgeable about the estate. Robert made a mental note to put him up top on his interview list.

Berdanier gulped water from his goblet and wiped a drip from his chin. "Excuse my poor word choice. Unless paperwork exists regarding this understanding, as you put it," he shrugged, "my point may have no bearing on a sales deal."

Katherine spoke up. "Micah, the estate appreciates your work. You have a home and the property it sits on as long as you want. That is if my say counts in the matter." She wrinkled her forehead and eyed Cameo.

Robert pinched his chin. The distance between mother and daughter extended beyond that of the seating at the table. Topazus complexities had loosened the lid on a boiling cauldron.

"I'm sure Chandler Developers will honor Micah's claim," Dean said.

"On your say so?" Berdanier snickered. "I reiterate. The heirs' property issue could kill a developer's interest in the property." Berdanier cocked his head toward Micah. "As you say, there have been seven generations, so undoubtedly more descendants exist than just you and your family. What can impede a sale is locating all the potential parties who could lay claim to the land and then reaching an agreement that satisfies all involved."

Katherine thrust her index finger toward Berdanier.

"You are looking for ways to stir things up unnecessarily and stop the sale."

James piped up again and directed his comment to Robert and Jane. "You can surmise from the fiery conversation, Topazus is well-named—the word derives from Greek, meaning fire. The estate has a reputation for heated conflict since the War Between the States when the feuding Clark brothers fought on opposite sides."

The guy seemed to know a little something about everything.

Rita continued to stir. "If there is financial concern, keep in mind that my catering business pays the estate a percentage when Topazus is used for receptions and weddings."

"Which is paltry compared to the financial need. In case the water isn't muddied enough, I support selling Topazus." Katherine said.

Rita snorted, and Dean suppressed a cough.

"Chandler Development boasts an incredible vision." Katherine surged forward. "They've offered to preserve what they can of the house and move it alongside the chapel and historical cedar tree. Continuing to patch this house," Katherine pointed to the walls, "and slap on paint and wallpaper, is pouring good money after bad. The developers can afford to restore it properly."

"But Topazus would pass out of the family." Cameo said.

Katherine whacked the table with her hand. "What difference does that make?"

"It's not what Daddy wanted," Cameo fired back. "And protecting the family heritage is why it was held in trust to begin with."

Katherine turned to Berdanier. "Remember, making wise investments is what *you* are to do." She thrust an admonishing finger at him.

"I'm trying to do the wise thing by keeping you informed." Berdanier waved his hand, wiggling his pinky ring at Katherine. "Don't shoot the messenger."

Katherine stood and stomped to the dining room door. She turned around, nostrils flaring. "I wouldn't bank on that request if I were you." She dropped the verbal bomb and the sound of her heavy departing footsteps echoed from the hallway.

So much for Cameo's perfect place to relax and unwind. Topazus may have outlived the Civil War, but could it survive the bitterness on display here today? Experience told Robert this Christmas vacation away from his "PI normal" would not be restful.

~

Jane set down her fork beside her half-eaten dessert. A pall covered the room. Luncheon plates had been cleared and lemon cheesecake served. Dining in this historic home had filled her dreams since Cameo extended the invitation to the plantation. But her dreams hadn't anticipated the quagmire she and Robert had stepped into.

Dean pushed back his chair and stood. "Excuse me. As Classic Realty's liaison for Chandler Development, I am presenting their Topazus vision at a meeting in Columbia later this afternoon. I had hoped to share the designer's proposals for this property with you. But now, all I can say is, keep an open mind about the company's offer." He directed his remarks to Cameo and Berdanier. "Thank you for lunch." He made a slight bow toward Rita and left.

The dessert lumped in Jane's stomach. Partially eaten cheesecakes rested on plates around the table except for Mr. Berdanier's. At present he was using his finger to lick his plate clean. She would have reprimanded her kindergarten students for showing such poor manners.

Berdanier leaned toward Robert and Jane. "You are being introduced to Topazus and the Clark family saga. My unenviable assignment as trustee is to handle the estate responsibly…" He drained his coffee cup, and it clattered against the saucer as he set it back down. "…which I will do." He folded and dropped his napkin on his dessert plate.

Jane placed her napkin beside her plate and instructed Robert. "Lay your used napkin beside the plate, not in it." She nodded toward Berdanier's bad example. "And don't refold it."

Micah had disappeared behind Mary Sue through the kitchen door, and James talked on his cell phone away from the table.

Berdanier picked at something lodged in a tooth. "Rita should offer toothpicks with her catering service," he muttered, but his voice carried throughout the room.

"So, Cameo," Berdanier said, "I guess it is best to let the dust settle on this foray. Let's meet in my office tomorrow. My reports are meant for your eyes only. But with a century-old house, one more day won't make a difference."

Rita interjected. "The house is one-hundred seventy-seven years old, closer to two centuries."

"I suppose, if you want to nitpick," he said, sucking at his tooth.

"And I do." She winced and looked down at her stylish tan shoes with narrow toes. "But like these shoes pinching my feet, it's not worth the hassle." She lifted a platter and limped her way to the kitchen.

Jane's feet twinged with empathy. She'd worn pointy-toed shoes like Rita's before and decided the looks did not outweigh the pain.

Berdanier shrugged. "I'll see you tomorrow?" he said to Cameo.

"Ten?"

"Ten it is." Berdanier left the dining room and walked into the hall where he sniffed ribboned cinnamon stick clusters on a Christmas tree.

Familiar with the Mobile attorney's punctuality, Jane predicted that Cameo might make the meeting by eleven. With the luncheon party scattered, she gave Robert a "what now" look.

Cameo took a last sip from her coffee cup and rose. "Robert, you and Jane join me in the library across the hall." I'll just be a few minutes." She took her cup to the kitchen.

"A few minutes?" Robert said. "We'll probably have time for a game of chess."

Jane snickered.

James passed by them, his ear to his cell phone, saying in a low voice, "Don't worry, you'll get your money." He ended his call and dropped the phone into his jacket pocket.

"Lovely luncheon." James rubbed his hands together and looked through the doorway. "Sorry you had to witness the discord." He lifted his chin, indicating Berdanier who was examining a vase in the great hall. "Enjoy your stay." He hurried toward the front door.

"I don't know if that directive is possible," Robert said. "Lead the way to the library."

"With pleasure." Jane stepped into the wide central hall that divided the Federal-style house, extending from the front entry to the back door. Since hearing about their assignment at Topazus, she had checked out books at the Mobile library and read internet articles about the house's history and printed off the floor plan. Off the main hall, the drawing room and library were on the right. On the left were the music room and dining room with an add-on kitchen. The original kitchen had been separate from the house as a precaution against fires.

Entering the library, Jane stared, unblinking, a moment. She took in the bookshelves that covered the library walls with a ladder on rollers providing a way to reach books shelved up to the ceiling. A Christmas tree stood in front of the window to the left and a small fire crackled in the fireplace on the right. Cozy.

"I could spend hours in this room." Filled with old books, the room carried a faint earthy scent tinged with cedar from the Christmas tree. Jane breathed deep, smelling memories. Many times, her brother and she put jigsaw puzzles together while a fire blazed in the family fireplace.

Robert scanned the room. "Looks like a place the men used to come to smoke."

"Could be," Cameo said. She arrived more quickly than Jane had imagined. "Topazus didn't have a dedicated smoking room popular in large homes of the period."

A massive desk designed with seating on both

sides commanded the room's center.

Cameo motioned for them to take a seat at the desk. "Sorry for the edgy conversation at lunch. But here's the deal. Family ownership has passed down from the original ancestors, Morgan and Martha Lee Clark, but stopped when my father married my mother instead of Rita as everyone expected. My grandfather, Stanford Clark, placed the estate in a trust with Torrance Berdanier. His son, Alfred who you met today, is successor trustee, and when his service ends, the management and control reverts to me."

"What is a successor trustee?" Jane asked.

"The person responsible for settling the trust for the beneficiary." She shrugged. "That's why I call him a middleman. My grandfather wanted to ensure that ownership bypassed my parents. I own the property, but the trust manages it. Since Daddy died, I've been busy with the law firm in Mobile and it has been easier for me to allow Berdanier to continue as trustee. But it may be time to pull his involvement. Mother has the right to live on and draw income from the property and voice her opinions only."

"Your mother mentioned living in a house on the hill."

"Yes. After Daddy retired and turned the law practice over to me, Mother had hoped to move back to Pine Bluff where they started married life and I grew up. But Daddy wanted to return to his roots. Mother agreed to live on the estate, but not in the plantation house. She said it made her head hurt. Building Crest Manor was the compromise."

Cameo's phone buzzed. She read the message, puffed out air and dropped her chin. "Dean is concerned about mother being upset and wants me to check on her." She pushed back from the desk. "She's not the only one upset." A frown creased her forehead. "Alfred Berdanier enjoys pressing people's buttons and went overboard today." She slapped her fist against the desktop. "He needs to be stopped." She stood, shoved the phone in her jacket pocket and strode toward the door. "Make yourselves comfortable. I'll be back shortly."

Jane squeezed her hands together, her eyes following Cameo. "Family dynamics bring out raw emotions."

"Ask any cop and he'll tell you domestic calls can be the most lethal. The love connection is powerful— along with its counterpart of hate and discontent."

Jane pursed her lips. "I can relate to the mixed feelings. My brother and I used to be close."

"Doesn't he live near here?"

"Outside Florence. He's an electrician and works with a remodeling and construction firm."

"You should invite him over while you're this close."

Her insides wilted. She shook her head. "What's the point? If he wouldn't come when mother was dying, I doubt he'd take time to see me."

"You won't know if you don't try."

She sighed as bitterness tapped her on the shoulder. Her brother, Adam, was the only close blood relative she had left. Her father had died in a construction accident after her parents divorced. Her mother, who died from cancer, had been gone six months. Sadly, she felt closer to those in the family cancer support group where she'd met Robert, than to her brother. "My heart says you're right. I've tried to push aside resentment, but ... I can't forget."

She dusted her hands together and stood, scanning the room. "For now, I'll enjoy Topazus." She turned all the way around. "All these books. All this history." Maybe her exposure to this room when she came with her aunt years ago is what sparked her bent for nostalgia. She ran her fingers along the spines of a matched set of history books. "If these books could talk, what would they say?"

"We're tired of being cooped up in here." Robert mimicked a high-pitched voice.

Jane sent him an eye roll.

Raising the corner of his mouth, he said, "What do you think they'd say?"

"I think they'd say, 'Come see what you can learn from me. Treasures are waiting to be discovered.'" Jane used her teacher voice.

"Hmm. A book filled with adventure and the good guy wins after guns blaze and horses whinny is my speed. I'm not all that big on flowery poems, classics, and such."

Jane reached for *The Last of the Mohicans* by James Fenimore Cooper. "Not all classics are as dull as you might think. Here's a good example." Jane brushed away a powdery gray haze on the cover and sneezed. "They should probably run a dehumidifier in here."

Jane pulled a tissue from her purse and wiped the cover. Opening the book, goosebumps tickled her neck. "This is a first edition. No telling what it's worth." She tapped the front. "The first hardbacks were made this way, using paper-covered boards."

"I recognize the title," Robert said, peering over

her shoulder. "What's it about?"

Jane read the summary page which spoke of wars, kidnapping, Indians, horses, guns, and gruesome conflict. "See? Adventure in abundance."

Cameo reentered the room. "Quite a collection, isn't it?"

Absorbed in book plots, it seemed she was gone a few minutes, but it had been close to thirty.

"Jane is trying to bestow me with a bit of culture." Robert returned to his seat and Jane shelved the classic. Patting the spine, the unique find sent another thrill through her.

Cheeks flushed, Cameo sat down in the desk chair and stared at her feet. Odd for her. After a moment, she straightened and inhaled deeply. "Sorry for the interruption. Berdanier's rudeness, innuendos and bullying has me unsettled." She tapped the desk. "Tell me. What have you found out about Chandler Development?"

"I ran a background on the company and the registered owner—a Mr. Reginald Wittmer. I found nothing amiss. No bankruptcy. No criminal charges. Credit scores are good." Robert touched his fingers making his points. "Dean Parsons acting on their behalf doesn't raise any red flags."

"Selling the plantation is not the legacy my grandfather wanted ..." Cameo choked on the words, and a pained expression crossed her face. She tilted her head upward. Keeping tears from spilling?

Jane hung her head in the uncomfortable silence. Having to deal with her mother's meager estate was challenging enough. Problems with a large plantation like Topazus must weigh heavy.

Robert sat and waited

Cameo sniffed. "Putting the estate in trust was grandfather's solution. But he dealt with Alfred's father, Torrance Berdanier, who is dead and gone."

Robert, steepled his fingers under his chin and gave Cameo a contemplative nod. "I can see the decisions you must deal with are—"

Heavy footsteps thudded down the hall. Jane turned toward the library entry as James surged into the room, eyes wide.

"Alfred Berdanier. He's dead."

CHAPTER TWO

A dead body is discovered, and Robert's whole being had reacted like a cop. He sat next to Jane in a Topazus electric cart with Cameo's heavy foot on the pedal. Air whipped his hair and adrenalin coursed through is blood. Following James' Jaguar, they sped along the long, wooded drive that stretched 150 yards from the mansion.

Reaching the plantation entrance, James pulled to the side of the drive and got out of his car.

A blue sedan sat angled into the exit gate.

James ran a shaky hand through his hair. "I called 911 as soon as I saw him." He sucked in air. "Berdanier was slumped over the wheel just like that." He gasped for another breath. "His car was still running. I reached in and turned off the ignition and then went back to tell you."

Robert stepped over to Berdanier's car, scrutinizing the situation.

"Heart attack?" Cameo asked from behind him.

Blood from a bullet wound in Berdanier's head trailed past his eye and pooled onto his shirt. "I don't think so. We better stay back until the police arrive."

On cue, a Bennett County Sheriff's car pulled up to the gate. Cameo opened the gate with the remote in the cart.

"I received a call. You have a death here?" The officer was young and by the looks of his shiny nameplate, D. Norwood, was fairly new to the force.

James shifted his weight from one foot to the other as he explained finding the body.

Officer Norwood bent down, resting his arms on the driver's open window and peered at Berdanier.

Robert cringed. Touching the vehicle could compromise evidence.

"A nasty bump on the head." Norwood stood and spoke to the group. "Had he been drinking?"

Robert's right eye muscle twitched, and he stepped forward. "Officer Norwood, the man has been shot."

The deputy pulled a pad and pen from his shirt pocket. "And your name?"

"Robert Grey with an e."

"I know how to spell Robert."

"My last name."

The officer wrote and then looked at him with one brow hitched up. "Okay. And how do you know this man has been shot?"

"He has a bullet wound to the head."

The officer leaned in for a closer look. "There does appear to be a singular hole." He straightened. "Likely suicide."

Robert gave him a sideward glance. Suicide? No visible weapon. Car pressed against the gate, still running. "First ..." Robert touched his right pointer finger to the left, then dropped his hands. The officer lacked insight and probably training. He searched for a few tactful words. "Do you have a crime scene investigator on call?"

"Not here. I work out of the annex office. I don't like to bother the sheriff's office unless it's absolutely necessary."

Robert swallowed. "I assure you it is necessary. They'll commend you for calling in support."

"I'll radio the main office to send someone."

"Perfect."

The officer went to his car. Robert's instincts for handling a crime scene kicked in. He did a cursory check for any spent shells or anything out of place. The briefcase in the passenger seat was closed, but one of the latches was open.

Norwood returned.

Robert asked. "Do you have any crime scene tape? I used to be in law enforcement and can help you cordon off the area."

"In the glove box," he said on the way back to his vehicle.

Jane pulled on Robert's sleeve and jerked her head towards the Jeep that pulled up. A young man dressed in a stiff collared shirt with a string tie was accompanied by a girl in a billowy pink gown.

"Docents," Cameo said. "'ll tell them the evening's event has been canceled and to pass the word."

"Good. The fewer people wandering around the better," Robert said.

"I'll call Rita. She'll need to inform her workers

too."

Officer Norwood carried a roll of yellow and black tape. "An investigator from the sheriff's office is on the way and they will contact SLED." He unfastened the tape. "They requested I secure the scene."

"Is that the South Carolina Law Enforcement Division?"

"Yes, sir."

"I've worked with them before."

"You were a state investigator?"

"In Alabama. I'm a private investigator now."

"Word is spreading about Berdanier," Jane said. "Rita and Micah are here now."

Rita wore a cook's apron over her dress. She had a pinched expression, probably no longer related to her shoes. Micah was solemn.

"All the more critical to secure this scene. Jane, keep them occupied if you can."

"Hand me the end of the tape," he said to Norwood. "Let's rope off the gate area."

Micah walked over to him and stopped at the tape. "Do you know what happened?"

"Only that Berdanier was shot, and he's dead. Investigators are on the way."

"It's hunting season. Could the shooting be from a stray bullet?" Micah asked.

"Possible. He doesn't appear to be shot from close range. The hole is clean with no visible powder burns, but forensics will make that determination."

Cameo had stayed with Jane, who had managed to keep Rita and James engaged away from the crime scene. She was becoming more valuable to him all the time. Micah went to speak to Katherine, who arrived with Dean in another Topazus cart. Wasn't Dean supposed to be on his way to Columbia?

Two officers in ties and jackets approached. Officer Norwood introduced Detective Chuck Johns from Bennett County Sheriff's Office. Johns introduced Investigator Jim Kelley from SLED. Behind them, a crime scene van pulled in. As a former agent with the Alabama Bureau of Investigation, Robert knew the routine. He needed to step back and let the crime scene specialists do their work evaluating and collecting physical evidence. A technician immediately began taking photos.

His insides collapsed. He was now relegated to the civilian side of the crime tape, a bystander. From experience in the ABI, a PI might earn the title of meddlesome bystander in the eyes of law enforcement.

But his pulse still rose as the specialists went to work. The pressing urgency to find answers quickly when a death occurred remained, even if he no longer carried a badge. Powerless, Robert kept his mouth shut. His gut hardened.

After the SLED investigator talked to James, he approached Robert. "I understand you're a private investigator. How did you get involved?"

Robert explained that he and his intern were guests of Cameo Clark and had been at the luncheon Berdanier just attended.

"Did anything unusual happen? Anything that might hint at someone wanting him dead?"

"The deceased didn't seem anxious. He brought up trustee issues he was prepared to discuss with Cameo who owns the estate."

"What issues?"

"Several. He mentioned insurance, a stolen ring, historic preservation to name a few. Berdanier and Cameo had agreed to meet at 10:00 a.m. tomorrow morning in his office."

Kelley's face was a blank sheet, like the page he flipped to in the notepad he held in his hand.

"Anything else?"

"I noticed a latch on Berdanier's briefcase was unfastened."

Kelley turned to the car where a CSI officer dusted for prints. "That will be noted."

"Here's my card. Contact me if you remember something that might be pertinent." He handed him a business card and moved on to speak to Micah.

Robert slid the card in his shirt pocket. He had done what he could and had a job to do for Cameo. He motioned to Jane. "Deputy Norwood looks like a wallflower at a dance. He's a local boy. Let's ask him some questions about the area."

They joined Norwood. He adjusted his gun belt. "I'm relieved the sheriff's men, SLED and CSI are here. Glad you suggested it."

Robert smiled. "I'm compiling information to help Ms. Clark make a decision about the future of Topazus. Can you tell me anything about the economy and growth in this area?"

"The Morgan Cotton Gin is really the only business of any size remaining in this part of Bennett County. With recent weather setbacks, the cotton industry has taken a hit."

The mention of weather detoured the conversation into several side bar stories. Robert's gift—to get people talking—was a critical factor in an investigation.

After hearing about the recent weather-related disasters, Robert steered the discussion back on track.

"Do you see a chance the economy will bounce back?"

"Maybe, but even then, most of the cotton produced will be exported because local textile factories are gone. Topazus with its December Christmas events brings in tourists, but historic downtown only contains a few small businesses. Now that Mr. Berdanier is gone, Morgan City won't even have an attorney."

Officer Kelley returned and motioned Robert aside. "I have interviewed those at the luncheon. The estate foreman said that there was talk of shooting squirrels and conflict over the sale of the property to a developer." He ran his finger down his notes. "And Attorney James Parsons said Katherine Clark left the luncheon early, and she threatened Berdanier."

Robert hesitated. He wanted his words to be accurate. "Katherine said she had trouble with squirrels and coons around her house and kept a rifle handy. As far as a threat … her comment was more of a retort. Berdanier had been presenting controversial issues and said, 'Don't shoot the messenger.' Katherine said something like … he shouldn't count on it."

Kelley underlined something on his notepad and flipped it closed. "Thanks. The coroner will transport the body to the Granite Ridge medical examiner's office." He turned and walked away but Norwood, still talkative, caught up with him.

When Robert joined Jane, she said, "We've all been excused. Rita left with Cameo on the cart we came in."

Micah called to Robert and hurried over. "James offered to give me a ride to my truck so I can drive to the cotton gin. Can you take the cart Rita and I came on back to the mansion?"

"No problem."

Robert got behind the wheel and Jane climbed onto the front seat next to him. A reindeer pinecone ornament dangled from the rearview mirror. "We made ornaments like these in my kindergarten class last year." Jane reached up and examined the decoration more closely. "The kids loved the project, but preparing the cones killed my hands."

Jane had shared with him that teaching hadn't been her plan for a career, but she had a special spark in her voice when she referred to her students. "You enjoyed working with the children, didn't you?"

"The children were fun. The demands put on teachers, not so much."

Robert's phone beeped. He reached for it, while backing up, jostling the cart.

Jane touched his arm. "Hold up. The box on the back seat tipped over." Jane jumped out.

Robert checked his phone. Cameo had texted:

Meet me at Berdanier's office in town ASAP.

Sliding back on the front seat, Jane said, "No harm done. A few spilled pinecones apparently prepped to make the reindeer ornaments. Don't lose anymore. I know how hard they are to cut."

"I'll try to be careful, but we are on an ASAP mission for Cameo. She wants us to meet her at Berdanier's office in town."

"Really? I wonder if she has a theory about what happened. She was distraught when she returned to the

32

library earlier."

"She'll tell us when she's ready."

Jane nodded and glanced back at the roped off murder scene "Poor fella'. At least he enjoyed his last meal."

~

Robert pulled in beside Cameo's Lexus.

"Is this legal, going into Berdanier's office?"

"It's not illegal. But if I was the state investigator, I wouldn't like people nosing around in the deceased's office. However, Cameo is the client." He thrust the car into park. "And she has a key."

The ground floor of the corner brick building housed Berdanier's office. A narrow set of stone steps led to the back door.

"You first," Robert said.

Jane clasped her hand to her throat. "Chivalry in the South is not dead. Or am I going first so you can say, 'She went in and I just followed her?'"

His shrug and grin told her she might have found him out, but he said, "I'm your backup. By the way, make backup the next rule on your list."

Her knees went weak. "You're a little late giving me that rule, aren't you?" Her impromptu romp in the woods when she followed a suspect by herself during their last case, led to her being gagged and bound like a calf in a rope tying contest.

"There are rules and then there is common sense. I didn't think I had to tell you not to trot off in the woods alone to go snooping."

"Am I going into a situation where I need a backup now?"

"Maybe not."

"Great."

She reached the top step and pulled out the notepad she kept in her purse, that Robert called luggage, and flipped pages. "We're on number six."

"Okay. Rule Number Six: In tenuous situations, always have a backup."

"Tenuous." She repeated with a dropping sensation to her stomach. "Fine. So, this is risky." She deposited her pad back into her purse and looked at his shoes.

"Did you change into running shoes in case we needed to leave in a hurry?" She meant every bit of her accusing tone.

"Not a bad idea. But no. Somehow greasy soot smudged my dress shoes, so I changed them."

Cameo opened the door. "Glad you're here. I've looked through a few folders on Alfred's desk, which is a challenge. He's the type who has his own filing system and stacked his papers accordingly."

She pointed to a large mahogany desk with scrolled trim, standing on legs with claw and ball feet. Not the desk Jane would have pictured Berdanier sitting behind.

"His desk is a beautiful Chippendale," Jane said. She ran her fingers over the trimmed edge.

"Fancy desk and oak file cabinets. Alfred enjoyed his antiques and cigars," Cameo said. "But when his father was alive, you'd smell sweet pipe tobacco and furniture polish in here instead of this acrid cigar smoke."

Jane examined a large chunk of stone with one side polished exposing shiny streaks of rose and gray. The other side was rough. "Interesting paper weight."

"Yup." Robert turned to Cameo. "How do you want to tackle the search?"

"See if there is anything on the computer." She pointed to the laptop on the credenza behind the desk. "Jane, look in the file cabinets. I'm interested in anything related to Topazus, the trust, and any issues Alfred brought up at lunch."

While Cameo muttered folder names she examined at the desk, Jane went to work, flipping through alphabetized files of agreements, cigar suppliers, contracts, estate planning, estate-Topazus. Ah. She pulled the folder filled with old newspaper clippings, leaflets and brochures advertising Topazus.

"Jane, any luck over there?" Robert asked.

"I found a file on Topazus spanning decades and historical information."

"Nothing to kill someone over?" Robert asked.

"Not to my untrained—"

The office door rattled open. Jane jerked her head toward the door.

Agent Kelley, accompanied by Detective Johns, stood there, head shaking in tsk-tsk fashion.

Jane, with her hand stuck between file folders, felt like a student caught pilfering the teacher's answer sheets.

"Well. We all meet again."

~

He'd had his back to the door and shouldn't have. Robert attempted a self-confident smile.

Cameo pushed the top drawer of the desk closed.

"How did you three get in here?" Officer Kelley's brows pinched together.

If Robert were in Kelley's shoes, he'd have a frown on his face too. Giving the appearance of opposition to law enforcement settled as a pain in the back of his throat. He should have encouraged Cameo to wait.

"If you're suggesting we broke in. We did not," Cameo said. "I have a key. Do you have a search warrant?"

"No. But we have a homicide."

"You've ruled out accidental death?" Robert asked.

Kelley glared at him. "What I've ruled is that when it's impractical and counterproductive to get a search warrant, it's my responsibility to prevent evidence from being altered or destroyed until I do obtain one."

Robert stood. "In all fairness I understand your concern, but I believe we are on the same team."

Officer Kelley planted his feet in a wide stance. "I need your cooperation. We have a job to do. You understand as a former state agent. Do you not?"

Robert held up his hands. "Of course. It's your case. My client felt compelled to locate and read the information her lawyer had compiled to discuss with her."

"All the more reason for your cooperation, since the information could relate to his death."

Robert nodded and pointed to the computer screen. "Items on his browser relating to Topazus were insurance for historic homes and heirs' property. He mentioned both at lunch."

Jane returned the file she had pulled and closed the file drawer. "I only found a folder regarding the estate's history."

Cameo slapped the file she was reviewing on the desk. "All I've found relates to heirs' property that Berdanier said at lunch he was ready to discuss."

"And was someone so determined that Berdanier be prevented from relaying that information, that he killed for it?" Kelley exhaled loudly. "It is to your benefit that we use our inherent duty to protect and secure the evidence that may be here."

"Understood." Robert said. "We'll leave you with it." He sent Cameo a look to not argue and hoped she took it to heart.

"If you have further information or questions, call me," Kelley said. "The crime scene specialists have finished their work at the estate."

"When is the autopsy report expected?"

Kelley looked to Deputy Johns. "The coroner said he'd try to have the results in the morning."

"We'll be in touch as needed. So, until then." The agent stepped aside, making the way clear for them to depart.

~

Cameo's remarks about Investigator Kelley were not complimentary.

Descending the steps from Berdanier's office, Robert could almost feel the steam emanating from her.

"I don't like kowtowing to him," Cameo muttered while marching to her car. "Pulling that inherent duty baloney."

"Look," Robert said, "the last thing you want is to alienate him. We'll make better progress by being cooperative. Trust me."

Jane stepped up. Pushing her long auburn hair off one shoulder, she flashed them a wide grin. "Robert, you were telling me about having a backup in tenuous situations?"

"Yes."

She held up a thumb drive. "Let's hope Berdanier followed that rule and backed up his reports."

CHAPTER THREE

On their return to Topazus, the cheery lights and wreath on the *Christmas at Topazus* sign belied the horror of the afternoon. Jane's dream visit had never included murder.

Berdanier, his BMW, and all other evidence of a murder scene had disappeared. Cameo punched in numbers on the security box, and the gate swung open. Robert followed behind Cameo on the winding drive that circled a wooded area accented with replicas of deer and angels illuminating the darkness. The break in trees gave way to Topazus.

Exiting their cars, Rita opened the front door to welcome them. Her classic portrayal of normal southern hospitality concealed the abnormal. "I was just finishing my inventory for the mother-daughter tea party in the morning and saw your headlights."

"You don't think you should call off the tea?" Cameo asked.

"The investigator said activities could resume since

the crime scene processing was complete."

"The death may affect attendance."

"Since we canceled this evening's lantern tour, I received calls asking if the events were called off but let them know tomorrow's events would resume."

While Cameo talked to Rita, Jane hung back with Robert and admired the wreath entwined with white lights that made the beveled glass surrounding the front door shimmer.

"You're a wonder Rita," Cameo said, "making this place come alive year after year."

Rita reached out and grasped Cameo's hands. "I treasure my moments here—the decorations, events, guests—I wouldn't give it up for anything." Her eyes glinted in the glow of the Christmas lights. Cameo and Rita entered the great hall and continued in conversation.

Jane stopped at the front door and inhaled the fresh woodsy scent of the decor. "Can't you feel the past? It's like stepping inside a history book."

"What I feel is the cold out here." Robert nudged her back. "Why not step inside and immerse yourself in all the history you want?"

"Oh. Sorry." She hurried inside, thankful for her employer-friend who put up with her fascination of antiquities. "It's curious that Cameo's mother didn't take on the role of decorating and hosting events rather than leaving it to her friend." Jane took in her surroundings. "If this was my family estate, I'd love to live here, but it seems to unnerve her."

"I agree. When Berdanier started bringing up issues that could impede the property sale, the woman's hands trembled to the point that she had to use both hands to steady her water goblet. She and Rita are definitely opposites when it comes to this house." He shrugged. "To each his own." He tilted his head down the hall. "We'd better catch up with Cameo."

"We were at Berdanier's office," Cameo was saying, "but the SLED officer came and asked us to leave. We came back here to hash over what has happened."

"I'll make tea before I go," Rita said.

"Don't go to any trouble." Cameo thrust up her hand. "You've already put in a long day."

"Oh, but I'd enjoy preparing a tray. You can sample some to the date squares I made for tomorrow's tea."

Jane had previewed the weekend activities listed in the brochure in her room. "I saw the events calendar," Jane said to Rita. "You have a busy day tomorrow starting with the mother-daughter tea and tours later in the day."

"You and Robert have a treat in store. Rita keeps my great-times-four-grandmother alive with her portrayal and knows her part to perfection."

Rita raised a wistful hand. "After over thirty years, Martha Lee is a part of me. So ... I'll be making your tea."

Lining the wide hall were settees of period furniture and paintings, some hung so high you had to crane your neck to see them. Much of the artwork depicted landscapes, but one of a lady drew Jane's attention. The woman wore a pale blue gown with white gloves that reached above the elbows. Light blond hair streaked with gray was pulled up with a tiara. Displayed on her gloved finger was the magnificent red topaz ring for which the estate was named. When Jane had visited years earlier with her aunt, the extraordinary ring was on exhibit in a glass case.

"Jane, you coming?" Cameo asked.

"You have to make allowances for a history buff." Robert gave Jane an amused smile.

"Sorry. The painting of your grandmother wearing the topaz ring is lovely. It's such a shame the ring was stolen."

"And ironically, the insurance payoff defrayed the hard-financial hits from ruined cotton crops."

"Your dig at Berdanier about insurance fraud, what was that about?" Robert asked.

"The insurance investigator inquired about our lax security and I didn't like being quizzed about it. Mostly, I wanted to let him know my distress over his management of the trust." With a brisk rub of her hands, she changed the subject and powered up the computer on the desk. "Let's see what you have acquired for us, Jane."

Jane reached in her pocket and handed her the drive.

"This computer doesn't have a lot of memory, but we'll try it."

The computer whirred into action.

Jane stepped over to the bookshelves and scanned the titles.

The scent from the Christmas tree did little to color the musty air around the fireplace. Even so, the scent of vintage books spoke of wisdom, knowledge, and adventure, giving Jane the same euphoria, she had when she was allowed in the library stacks at the University of Alabama to work on a research paper.

She trailed over a section of how-tos—embroidery stitches, quilting, tree cutting, building your own log cabin. *Ledger*. Jane lifted the worn green book with gold lettering from the shelf and turned to the title page, bronze with age. Handwritten on the inside cover in ink was "Morgan D. Clark." Did this book belong to the original Topazus owner? A few loose pages poked out.

"Finally. Here's a list of documents," Cameo said.

Jane tucked the loose pages back and returned the book to the shelf.

Rita entered with a tray. "I prepared a pot of hot water to make tea or hot chocolate and added some finger sandwiches along with the date bars." She blew at a strand of hair pestering her eye.

"Thank you," Cameo said. "Catering is definitely your forté."

"On the desk by the computer all right?" She leaned to view the screen. "Find something at Berdanier's office?"

"A drive. Maybe we'll find the reports he talked about at lunch."

"Ah." Rita peered over Cameo's shoulder. "Good luck. He apparently had a host of topics to discuss." She frowned at the list of documents displayed on the screen.

"Here's a document titled, meeting topics." Cameo clicked on the item.

Rita hung the errant strand of hair behind her ear. "Cameo, you should check on your mother. She was agitated today and … well, I've known her to fly off the handle."

"Don't worry. I'll check on her before bed."

"Okay. I better run. I still have to go to the store."

Rita hurried from the room.

Cameo clicked the mouse again. "The computer evidently can't read that file. I'll try a different one."

"How did Rita become so devoted to Topazus?" Robert asked.

"Looks like it's trying to load … huh?"

"Rita. I was curious about her interest in Topazus."

Cameo frowned, clicked the mouse again and sat back in the desk chair, keeping her eyes on the computer screen. "Well, Rita and my dad were high school sweethearts. She expected and prepared to become the mistress of Topazus. When my mother's family moved here, Rita recruited mother as a Belle. My dad fell for the new girl. After high school, instead of pursuing agribusiness at Clemson as planned, my Dad ended up in law school at the University of Alabama where my mother attended."

Jane gave an approving nod. "Your mom and dad made a wise college choice."

Robert folded his arms in front of him. "Said the dedicated Roll Tide graduate."

Cameo chuckled. "Dedicated describes Alabama fans. Mom and Dad bonded at UA and married after graduation. Not long after, Rita married Dean. She started her catering business and took over the training of the Belles and Beaus tour guides."

"How does Rita involve Topazus in her catering?" Jane asked.

"When Rita uses Topazus for wedding receptions, luncheons and other special events including the preparation of breakfast for plantation guests, she pays fifteen percent of her profits to the estate. At Christmas all proceeds from admissions go to the estate, Rita donates her time with the home and tour events. My mother plans the crafts and outdoor activities."

The romantic betrayal of Cameo's father by selecting Katherine must have been a blow to Rita. But she seemed to have compensated by centering her business and volunteer work around the estate. "Interesting how they've worked things out," Jane said.

"When I was little, I asked mother why she didn't play the part of the mistress. Her answer, I've never forgotten. 'The house,' she'd said, 'troubles me. I enjoy visiting, and letting you play the role of little sister in the pageant. I love the gardens and the chapel, but there is something about the house that rejects me.'"

"Strange. I've never heard of a house not liking someone," Jane said.

"It seemed odd to me too." Cameo gave the computer keys extra clicks. "She said it was the feel of the walls. In Crest Manor she feels hugged, but Topazus' walls and even the topaz ring gave her a cold shoulder."

"All this is interesting, but shouldn't we be looking at what's on the drive?" Robert asked.

"Yes, but … now the computer's locked up."

Robert circled the desk and looked at the screen. "You could reboot, but the software probably needs to be updated."

Cameo dug in her purse. "My phone is charging in my room and James is supposed to call. I'll go get my phone and my laptop. Maybe the drive will work on it. Help yourself to the tea items. I'll be right back."

Jane poured tea, and Robert opted for hot chocolate. She grasped her teacup, glanced around the room, and was transported—the books, the tree trimmed in natural strands of popcorn and cranberries, and Civil War tea service. She laughed.

Robert smiled. "A confederate buck for your thoughts."

"Aunt Bessie Lawrence from Florence."

"Sounds like the beginning of a limerick."

Jane giggled. "It was the pet name my brother and I gave our aunt."

"Is she still in Florence?"

Jane shook her head. "She died in a car accident a couple of years ago. Hard to believe, but it has been over twenty years since she brought me here." But when she did," Jane held her cup with her little finger lifted and wiggled the ring finger on her other hand. "I was Scarlet O'Hara in a red dress blinding my beaus with the fire from the topaz."

"Your beaus were plentiful?" The side of his mouth lifted.

"Uh … no … unless the cad I dated through college before he dumped me, and my self-absorbed assistant principal count." She stretched her neck, then glanced at the simple ring on her finger dull in comparison to the Topazus ring and laughed at her own antics. "Maybe that computer drive will have information about the topaz ring since an issue was made about the insurance payoff."

There was a rustling. Jane couldn't tell which direction the sound came from. "Did you hear that?"

"Guess not. What did you hear?"

"A swishing sound coming from …" Jane walked to the center of the room. "… I'm not sure."

Robert walked over and sat on the edge of the desk.

"The power of suggestion has you hearing Katherine's unfriendly walls."

"Now you're making fun, but there was a noise."

Footsteps sounded in the hall and Cameo breezed in.

"Maybe it was the anticipation of Cameo's arrival you heard." Robert hitched a lopsided grin and moved off the desk.

"James called and should be here shortly," Cameo said. "Let's try the drive on this computer."

Cameo set up her computer beside the other one and plugged in the drive. Jane moved with Robert behind Cameo to view the screen.

"Here we go." She clicked on the USB drive and pulled up the download listing. "Jane, jot these down."

Jane pulled the notepad from her purse and started writing while Cameo read aloud. "Finding heirs' property, historic preservation rights, thousand-year flood, Myrtle Beach Pawn, mineral rights, Topazus insurance claim 09-25-2018. Ah. Here's a file titled 'list of concerns for Cameo,' dated just three days ago."

Cameo opened the document, then slapped the desk. "And that's what it is, another list."

"It must be the items Berdanier was ready to report on." Robert ran his finger down the list, reading it out loud. "Income in the red: cotton crops, impact of weather events, Christmas celebration revenues; Katherine, Dean and Chandler Development; mold issue; historic preservation; Heirs' Property claims; and THE RING."

Cameo tapped the screen. "Interesting. It's written in all caps."

Jane was in the middle of writing 'the ring' when

the lights went out.

~

Robert could barely see his hand in front of his face.

"Stay still. I know where the fuse box is," Cameo said.

Robert fished his phone from his pocket and tapped the flashlight app. "Here, use this." Cameo went into the hall.

Ahchoo!

"Bless you," Robert said.

"I didn't sneeze," Jane said. "It must have been Cameo."

A light scraping noise came from the fireplace area. "Now you've got me hearing noises."

"This place is spooky in the dark," Jane said.

"The window curtains are drawn." Robert inched his way to the windows, grasping furniture to help feel his way across the room.

"Ouch. That's my foot," Jane said.

"Now you're feeling things too? I'm nowhere near you." Robert reached the heavy textured drapes and pulled a section back, letting in moonlight that slightly illuminated the books and furnishings. Jane was standing where he'd left her.

"Something or someone hit my foot." Jane's tone was insistent.

"Hello?" A man's voice.

A light shone in the hall.

"James?" Cameo called out. "Down here. I'm looking behind the paintings for the fuse box."

James passed the library doorway. His lantern-style flashlight cast enough residual light into the room to maneuver.

Robert walked to the doorway, Jane on his heels. "You came at a good time. We've been groping in the dark."

"Won't be the first time this has happened," James said. "These old fuses blow every so often. I just saw Micah outside fiddling with extension cords. Could have something to do with the lights going out." He held the light up higher and pointed. "Cameo, the box is down here."

"I was close." Cameo said.

James removed a framed picture from the wall. "We're dealing with the extra Christmas lights coupled with old wiring. Micah keeps extra fuses handy." In seconds, the lights came on. James replaced the picture, and they filed back into the library.

Cameo nudged Robert and returned his phone.

Jane went back to the computer, then took a step back.

"The computer drive. It's gone."

CHAPTER FOUR

Who killed Berdanier? Who stepped on her foot? Who stole the computer drive? Mold, a stolen ring, property disputes. She and Robert had talked and talked. A compelling mystery. But as Robert reminded her, none of the death investigation was their business. Only information on Chandler Development.

So, cotton crops, preservation and property claims weren't responsible for keeping her awake. It was not hearing from Adam. She had called her brother and left a message with Bethany, her sister-in-law, explaining the electrical work needed at Topazus. She'd asked for Adam return her call. But he had not texted or called.

Jane took a bite of vegetable omelet and admired the pink rose on the breakfast tray sent from the Topazus kitchen. She was supposed to be here to relax. Berdanier and estate issues–not her problem. She reached for the novel she'd been reading.

The phone rang. Adam?

"This is Rita. Sorry to disturb you so early, but the

Belle who assists with the mother-daughter tea called in sick. Cameo would normally be my sub, but she left with James for the coroner's office. Would you be willing to play the role of my cousin Camilla from Boston and serve tea?"

Would she? She moved the tray and bounced off the bed. "Gee, yes. I'd love to."

After making quick work of her breakfast and showering, she joined Rita upstairs in the mansion.

Dressing Jane in a corset, fitted bodice with puffed sleeves, and a skirt with a petticoat and hoop cage underneath, Rita explained the morning event. "Mothers make reservations far in advance for their daughters to learn proper tea etiquette in the classic setting that Topazus offers."

Leading the way to the dining room, Rita clarified Jane's responsibilities and taught her how to sit in a hoop skirt. "Catch a rib of the hoop cage and lift it slightly, then sit."

Rita wore a blue gown, much like the one Martha Lee Clark wore in her portrait. A reproduction of the Topazus ring gleamed on Rita's left hand, but the stone was not as brilliant as the original.

Soon, twelve guests wearing velvets and taffeta in festive Christmas colors lined the sides of the dining table with Rita and Jane occupying the end seats. When Rita nodded Jane stood to serve the tea.

Jane's hand trembled, lifting the teapot to pour the fragrant floral tea into delicate china teacups. She prayed silently. *Lord, this may seem a strange request but please don't let me spill or break anything.*

Rita, completely in character as Martha Lee Clark, removed the monogrammed napkin from the silver holder and with a flick of the wrist, placed the linen in her lap and twelve napkins followed suit. She demonstrated how to handle butter and explained optional ways to prepare their tea by adding cream, or lemon and sugar.

When Martha Lee—Jane now experienced Rita as her character—began to compare the tea crumpet to the English muffin, Jane settled down and remembered the tea party she had arranged for her brother, her favorite doll, and Mr. Bear.

Adam was four years older and she revered him. She looked to him to see if a joke should be laughed at or shrugged off. The foods he liked became her favorites. Her veneration extended to mimicking his movements when he talked, walked, and sat down. She especially adored him when he tolerated her tea parties and let her play with his matchbox cars. They had been close then.

Jane lifted a crumpet. Adam's plastic Legos had made fine tea cakes. A year later they were ripped apart by their parent's divorce. She'd begged her brother to come with her, but he'd chosen to stay with their father.

With tea etiquette and foods explained, Martha Lee shared the history of the Topazus name. "Ladies, I am pleased to share my home with you during this marvelous Christmas season. My husband, Morgan Clark, built Topazus. The estate's name derives from the word topas or tapaz, meaning fire in Sanskrit, the ancient language of India. The name later became attached to an island in the Red Sea." She gave a wave of her hand. "But that is another story."

She fluttered the fingers on her left hand. "This ring is the inspiration for the plantation home and grounds." She crossed her hands on her chest. The gem caught the light from the chandelier. "My husband, ever the adventurer, sojourned with Brazilian natives where he mined this stone. Brazil produces the finest, most vibrant and valuable red topaz which is incredibly rare. He presented me with this topaz surrounded by diamonds for our third wedding anniversary. And that is when the foundation of this home was laid." She opened both hands to face the ceiling. "And a year later Topazus, as you see it today, was complete."

Jane wanted to clap.

"But enough about me. Please Camilla, you begin. Then each of you tell your name and little about yourself."

Jane straightened, cleared her throat, and attempted to take a deep breath but was hampered by the corset. "I am Camilla, Martha Lee's cousin from Boston. I always enjoy my visits to Topazus. When I was your age, I prepared tea parties for my dolls and stuffed animals." One of the little girls giggled and her mother shushed her. "Now I am pleased to join each of you for tea this morning."

The mothers took turns introducing their daughters, and after some rather stilted conversation, Martha Lee put them out of their misery. "Ladies, it would be my pleasure to have you see my home." She ushered her visitors to the great hall and began the tour.

Jane stole a quick look at her silenced phone and checked text messages to see if her brother might have responded. Nothing.

After the tour Martha Lee said, "Camilla, will you direct our guests to the area set up for crafts?"

"Certainly." Jane delivered her next set of lines.

"Another yearly Topazus tradition is making an ornament for you to take home and put on your own Christmas tree. Come this way." Jane lifted her hoop slightly as Rita had shown her and led the guests to the pavilion where Belles and Beaus were ready for them.

She checked her phone messages again.

"Antebellum ladies use cell phones?"

Adam stood in front of her.

Jane's eyes teared up at the sight of him. "You came."

He gave his head a shake, and a pained expression crossed his face. "I'm sorry I've given you reason to doubt I'd come."

She grabbed his arms. "I'm glad you're here now."

They hugged. Then he held her shoulders at arm's length. It had been six months since seeing him at their mother's funeral. He seemed … weary. She would be at Topazus for only a short time. Would it be long enough to repair their strained relationship?

"I hear you're a private investigator."

"That's PI intern, a big difference. It's a job I took while I take care of mother's affairs and sell her house. I'll go back to teaching next fall."

His eyes darkened, and he dropped his head. "I know I've been no help but—"

An understatement. The need to hear his explanation burned inside her but now was not the time. "Did Bethany tell you about the lawyer that was killed here yesterday?"

"She did. And it made the news in the Florence paper."

"The focus here is to continue the Christmas events while cooperating with the death investigation. But a power outage last night and a nonfunctioning outlet are creating problems. I   hoped—"

"I'll do what I can. Tuesday is my normal day off, so you were lucky I was working close by and able to cut loose for a little while."

So much for their reunion. He had pulled himself away from his busy schedule just like he'd done with the funeral. He shouldn't have bothered. Their mother wanted to see him when she was alive, not dead. The same hurt and anger she had experienced towards him at the funeral rose inside of her, like steam building in a teakettle. Little wonder he'd be slow to warm up to her. The wedge between them would require work to overcome on both their parts.

"Do you know where the power box is?"

She hung on her cheerful face. "That I know. It's behind a picture in the main hall."

Micah pulled up on one of the electric carts. "I saw the truck out front. Is electrical help here?" Rita wearing a full apron over her gown stepped from the kitchen utility porch.

After introductions, Rita went back in the kitchen. Jane stayed with Adam and Micah as they conferred and rerouted some Christmas light extension cords to the bed-and-breakfast which had newer electric lines.

"I think things will run smoothly with our changes and fresh fuses." Adam said. "Now, where is the nonfunctioning outlet?"

Jane led him into the dining room. The table had been cleared. "We had a lovely tea in here this morning." She pointed to the bad outlet, and Adam pulled out a screwdriver to remove the cover. "Remember the tea parties I used to hostess?"

"Yep. You and me, and your dolls."

"Those were happier times. Before the big divide."

"Um ..." He turned his back and went to work unscrewing the wall plate.

Um? That's it? She'd thrown out a remembrance. Wasn't it his turn? Now what?

Jane don't think on the negatives.

But the bad vibes pressed in. He had refused to visit Mom when she lay dying. How could he have done that?

Take the boiling teakettle off the heat.

He'd turned his back and was all business. She could be all business too.

When Adam removed the cover and held the outlet tester to the plug, the entire socket disappeared behind the wall, leaving a hole.

"What happened?"

Adam pulled out his flashlight and peered in. "There's a passage or compartment behind this wall. I discovered a chamber like this in another antebellum home."

He stood, running his hand over the wall. "There should be an access door." He explored the fireplace trim, then examined the fire brick. "Here. A brick with no mortar."

He slid the brick out to reveal a button, pressed it, and a concealed door in the wall popped open.

"Amazing," Jane whispered. The stripe of the wallpaper aligned perfectly with the door's edge.

Adam used his flashlight and stepped in. Jane peeked in behind him. The musty space appeared to be about four feet wide and ran behind the fireplace.

"The ceiling has a serious leak." Sheetrock sagged

above him. His flashlight exposed wallboard covered with black mold. He pointed the beam to the damp floor, littered with droppings. "They have a rodent problem too."

An answer for the scurrying noise? And was there another hidden space that played a role in mysterious disappearance of the computer drive? "I heard rustling in the library across the hall last night when the lights went out."

"Rats are nocturnal creatures. You probably heard them running the walls."

An involuntary shiver ran up Jane's spine. Were these rats heavy enough to stomp on toes?

"A person experienced with pest extermination and mold removal should be contacted, and repairs made. For now, I'll see if I can get this plug working." Adam picked up the outlet and examined the wires leading to it. "Frayed. Rodents love to chew on the coverings." He pulled out black electricians' tape and began wrapping the wires.

At yesterday's luncheon, Rita had said the man who did the mold inspection gave the house a clean bill of health. Either he didn't know what he was doing, or the mold problem was being covered up. Berdanier said he would have his own inspection done. But did anyone realize they had a rat problem? Different parties involved with Topazus seemed to have different agendas. Not her business.

With the plug reassembled, Adam retested it. "There's power to it now. Hand me that cord and we'll see what happens."

White lights on garland greenery sprang to life. The reflection on the massive mirror over the buffet gave the room a warm appeal unlike the musty mess hidden behind the wall. Lights like these had been Adam's job to troubleshoot while decorating the Christmas tree when their family was still together. Maybe the Christmas celebration could be a place for them to start over.

Adam pushed the recently discovered door back into place. "That should put things in order for the evening's events."

"There is a Christmas celebration tonight and a historical tour Sunday afternoon. Why don't you come with Bethany and the boys?"

"I can't tonight. We have the company Christmas party. But I'll try to make it Sunday." He gathered his tools and checked his watch. "I have another job."

He squashed her hope again.

Rita entered the dining room.

"Wonderful. The lights are on. You are a miracle worker. Can you send an invoice?"

"Yes, ma'am. But this is a temporary fix. The frayed wires should be replaced. And it's imperative the moisture, mold and rats behind the wall be addressed."

"What?" Her eyes widened and her hand went to her throat. "Behind the wall?"

Rita appeared shocked. Or was she troubled the space was uncovered?

~

Jane swallowed her disappointment after Adam left. Their meeting had been cordial but more business than a reconnection. Maybe childhood remembrances were meant to be just that—memories relegated to the past. Long ago happenings did nothing to answer the question of how the brother she had adored and who always had her back had changed so much.

The phone tucked in her waistband vibrated. A text from Robert.

Meet me behind the kitchen. Agent Kelley just served a search warrant at Crest Manor.

Jane hitched her dress off the floor and hurried through the dining room and kitchen. Women in the 1800s had to stay fit just to wear the cumbersome clothing that made it hard to not only to breathe but walk.

Robert stood on the kitchen porch, which served as a mud room and storage for cleaning and gardening supplies. Rita had a small office space opposite a garden bench with tools, gloves and clogs.

"You look like you stepped from the *Gone with the Wind* movie set." Robert said.

"Uh huh." She grabbed her ribcage. "That's 'cause Rita squeezed the wind out of me when she laced me into this corset. Reliving history is fascinating, but I'm grateful the fashions have changed." She squirmed in the bodice. "I can't take a full breath, and this hoop hinders me like a kindergartener in a sack race. What's this about a search warrant?"

"The SLED investigator convinced a judge he has grounds to search Crest Manor. The autopsy revealed that Berdanier was shot with a .22. "

"Oh boy. Is that the kind of gun used for squirrels and coons?"

"You've got it. The warrant states there is reason to believe that Katherine Clark is in possession of a .22 rifle and ammunition that could be evidence in the commission of a crime."

"Poor Katherine. What about the deer hunter

theory?"

"Deer hunters don't use a .22. They generally use a higher caliber firearm.

"A .22 can kill a person?"

"Oh yes. A .22 can be deadly. It's the weapon of choice for some contract killers."

"Even so. Just because she shoots squirrels, they can investigate her for murder?"

"In this case, yes. Go change and meet me at my truck. Cameo wants us to join her at Crest Manor. We've been officially pressed into service."

Jane hurried to the stairs and hiked up her skirts as she climbed to the second floor. Rita reserved the bedroom directly over the library as the wardrobe room for those playing roles in the Topazus events.

Rita stood at the window, her back to Jane. She held a gloved hand up, letting the ring catch the sunlight. The stone refracted flashes of brilliant light that danced on the walls. Rita was speaking. Jane could only catch some words. "... fiery light ... treasure ... built for me ... visitors ..."

Was she reciting lines for this evening's tour? Jane cleared her throat. "Um ... Rita, I need to change clothes. Robert and I have to meet Cameo. A search warrant has been served at Crest Manor."

Rita turned; her hands clasped. She stared, then blinked. "What did you say?"

"Agent Kelley served Katherine with a search warrant. I'm going with Robert to meet Cameo at Crest Manor." Jane unhooked the skirt, petticoat and hoop Velcroed at the waist. The garments dropped to floor, and she stepped out.

"Unacceptable." Rita scowled at Jane.

Unacceptable?

Still in the blue gown, Rita began to pace. She peeled off the elbow-length gloves, carefully rolling them with the ring inside, and placed them on the dresser. She faced Jane; her eyes adamant. "Get dressed, meet with the authorities and explain that nothing must interfere with tonight's festivities."

Jane's breath constricted more. "I can't tell law enforcement what to do. But I'll let Cameo know your concerns."

"My dear Jane," her tone shifted to solicitous. "Don't sell yourself short. You are a bright girl. Go do what you can."

Rita placed a lot more faith in Jane's investigator role than she should. "I suppose I can let them know you'd like to remain open." Her mouth dry and stomach queasy, she turned her back to Rita. "Could you release me from this corset?"

"Certainly. You did a fine job this morning and I thank you for asking your brother to work on electrical problems." Rita untied the corset as she spoke.

Relief.

Jane inhaled the air sweetened with the lavender potpourri. "Ah. It feels so good to take a deep breath. It's no wonder women swooned in historical novels."

Rita waved dismissive hands. "It feels like a second skin to me. The Christmas season events at Topazus must not be changed again. Financially, last night's closure was bad enough." She grabbed the skirts from the floor and hung them on a rack.

"The December celebrations help keep the estate running?"

"Absolutely. If we can salvage this season with a

good turnout, we'll make do."

Jane reached for her jeans and sweatshirt. "Do you think the murder at the front gate will keep people away?"

"A valid point but this business is built on visitors who have made coming here a family tradition. As long as we can stay open, I believe people will come. Everyone came to the tea and the crafts and tours are running smoothly."

Odd. Her entire focus was on Topazus business. Absent was any distress or shock that one might expect over the predicament Katherine faced. "Aren't you surprised about the search warrant and what it suggests?"

Rita raised her chin. "What does it suggest?" She spoke as if the question was an affront.

"That the murder weapon might be at Crest manor. And if it is, the murder suspect would likely be Katherine."

Rita pinched the bridge of her nose. "You're worried my concerns are misplaced?" She patted Jane's hand. "I still think the bullet that killed Berdanier was a stray shot. He was in the wrong place at the wrong time. Let the police serve their warrant, ask their questions, and do their job. I'm sure they'll figure it out."

"I hope you're right. What time are the evening events?"

"Craft and garden tours are over at two. Gates re-open at five-thirty."

She used her hand like a whisk broom, shooing her out of the room. "You run along now and make it known that the investigation mustn't curtail our activities. And tell that investigator we want no blue bubble lights. We must have Christmas lights only."

CHAPTER FIVE

Climbing the hill to Crest Manor in his truck, Jane filled Robert in on the instructions from Rita and her brother's discovery of rats and mold.

"Huh. So, there is reason for concern about mold?"

"Yes. Rita seemed surprised at his discovery of the secret passage behind the wall and the moldy mess."

"Water leaks, and rats running the walls present an unpleasant surprise but that issue will have to wait. This search warrant takes priority."

After ringing the bell, Cameo invited them in.

The home had an open plan with floor to ceiling windows in the great room giving view to the woods and a rocky bluff. He was a part of nature. "Incredible. This is quite a contrast to the formal environment of Topazus."

Cameo smiled. "If everyone liked the same thing, it would be a dull world. Mother is in the breakfast room."

They entered a large kitchen with a work island

and breakfast nook in the bay window. Mrs. Clark sat at a small dining table, her jaw set.

"Hello Mrs. Clark," Robert said.

"Call me Katherine." She spoke as if calling her Mrs. Clark was an irritation. She pushed her hair from her face, but the silver streak flopped back across her forehead. "Have a seat."

He and Jane took seats across from her. Cameo sat next to her mother.

Katherine frowned and exhibited an incongruous smile. "You tell them the total truth, be as open and honest as you can, and you're thanked by having your home invaded."

"It's how the system works, Mom."

"I never thought anyone could think I would kill." She slammed her coffee mug to the table, sloshing some of its contents. She grabbed a napkin and dabbed at the spill. "The only thing I've used that gun for is on pesky coons and the blasted squirrels that tear up my feeders." She pointed out the window to bird feeders hanging from a low tree limb.

"I explained to Mom that no matter how innocent you are, once officers turn up with official paperwork it's best to remain tight-lipped."

Katherine sniffed and slumped against her chair back, crossing her arms.

Robert nodded. "Lawmen love to have a suspect volunteer information, but Cameo is right. Could I see the warrant?"

Cameo handed the paper to him. He held it for Jane to see. It read:

Proof by affidavit of Agent J. R. Kelley, South Carolina Law Enforcement Division, I am satisfied there is probable cause to believe that on the premises of Crest Manor on Topazus Trail_inside the Topazus Estate on County Road 2032 in the County of Bennett in the State of South Carolina, there is now being possessed a .22 firearm and ammunition that was used as a means of committing a felony.

No question. Both he and Cameo were aware that Agent Kelley had locked onto Katherine as a suspect. The best help he could offer was a straightforward assessment. "What they will do next is conduct a forensic firearm examination in which specialists link bullets and cartridges to weapons, and weapons to individuals," Robert said.

Katherine leaned her forearms against the table. "So, I murder a guy. Bring the gun back. Prop it up by my back door. And not only don't conceal the weapon, but point it out to the officer when he comes to interview me?" She poked herself in the chest. "Do I really look that stupid?"

Her tone accentuated her frustration. All Robert could offer was insight into the law enforcement side and from Cameo's pensive expression that is what she wanted him to do. "Officers are supposed to collect evidence and facts and report what they find. Once the facts are gathered then reasons and motives for what is discovered can be explored. Right now, this warrant shows me the bullet that killed Berdanier was a .22. They would naturally want to test any .22 near the scene of the crime as part of their due diligence. That being said," he handed the warrant back to Cameo, "offering more information than is necessary may unfortunately increase suspicion, where you thought it would be seen as cooperation."

Katherine's lip muscles tightened.

"Do you mind telling me what you told them when they interviewed you?" Robert asked.

She shrugged. "More than I should have, apparently." She pushed the hair off her forehead but it slid back down. "I told the investigator that I left the luncheon irritated with Berdanier." She stuck up fingers to count. "First, for his obnoxious table manners and second for his condescending attitude. Dropping hints about sensitive issues and punching people's buttons …" She slapped the table. "I know I shouldn't have let him get to me, but he did. The man is infuriating … or was."

Lifting her chin, Katherine said, "I made my catty remark to him, and it felt good to walk out. Topazus stifles me. I told the officer that I needed fresh air when I left dining room. I walked to my house, but instead of entering, I took the path to the river."

"Did you see or speak to anyone?"

"He asked me that too. No. This house and pathway are isolated. People don't just happen up here. Except I saw Cameo in the circular drive when I returned."

"I can verify mother was coming up the river walk. When I arrived, I checked the house and went back to the cart to check the river trail when I saw her out back. We talked for a few minutes and I returned to the library."

"Did you notice the gun?" Robert asked Cameo.

"Um … yes … Mother was picking it up from the ground."

"Normally I keep the gun inside the screened porch next to the patio. I noticed the gun had fallen in the ashes. I had left it propped by the house outside after the coons flipped the grill and thought I'd better take it inside."

"May we see the porch?"

"Sure."

The screened porch provided a cozy area with wicker furniture and a swing that overlooked the patio and grill. Spilled ashes and charcoal remained on the ground outside. Robert took in the scene as Katherine pointed to the gun's locations beside the grill and then by the porch door.

"Honesty is normally the best policy," Robert said. "Hopefully, that will prove to be true in this case. Once your gun is test fired, we'll know more about where things stand in the investigation."

~

Inside the screened porch, Jane's superficial assignment from Rita played on her nerves. *You run along now and make it known that the investigation mustn't curtail our activities.*

"Uh … I don't know if now is the appropriate time," Jane began, "but Rita asked if this search would affect the Christmas event this evening."

Katherine swatted the air. "Of course, that would be Rita's concern."

"Mom. No need to get worked up. It's a natural question."

"We could experience an alien invasion and Rita's first thought would be: How will this affect me and Topazus?" Her tone mocking.

Cameo's phone buzzed. She checked the screen. "It's Rita. Excuse me." Cameo stepped onto the patio to take the call.

Katherine muttered. "Morgan and I never should have come back here. I only agreed to move if we didn't have to live in that god-forsaken house."

Jane shifted her feet and gave Robert a sidelong glance. She didn't know if she should comment or not. Katherine's remark was to the room at large, yet she and Robert could obviously hear her.

Maybe try a different subject. "You have lovely Christmas decorations in your home. Do you participate with the plantation crafts?" Jane asked.

"Outside events I enjoy. Anything to do with the Topazus house I leave to Rita. Most of the ornaments on my tree were handcrafted during the December celebrations. Come." Robert and Jane followed her into the living room with the glass wall, making it feel as though they were stepping outside.

"This tree is a live red cedar from the property," Katherine said.

Jane inhaled. "I love the smell."

"A reindeer." Robert pointed, "like the one in the electric cart."

"One of this year's crafts." Katherine unhooked the ornament. "I just prepared a box full of these pinecones."

"You'll be happy to hear that Jane rescued some of the critters during a crazy cart ride with a wild driver." Robert's self-deprecation brought a tad of levity to the Christmas merriment that had turned gloomy.

Katherine turned to Jane, "How's that?"

Jane chuckled and touched the prickly cone with the fuzzy pipe cleaner antlers. "The box fell from the cart Robert was driving, but I retrieved those that spilled."

"She let me know that prepping the cones comes at great sacrifice to the hands." Robert winced and wiggled his fingers.

Katherine grinned. "I've worked out a technique." She held up the ornament. "Since the top of the cone forms the head, I locate the base of the head, then snip away a couple of rows of scales using needle nose pliers. That exposes the center, then it's easy to cut with a craft saw."

"Brilliant." Jane whacked her own forehead with the heel of her hand. "The secret is clearing the scales. My fingers were raw after preparing twenty-five pinecones."

Cameo joined them. "Mother is clever—when it comes to decorations."

Jane wasn't sure if she meant the comment as a compliment or to emphasize that her mother's efforts were limited compared to running the show at Topazus as Rita did. Or was she pointing out the unclever way her mother handled police questioning? Katherine lost her glow and rehung the ornament.

"Rita says some cancellations from the Belles and Beaus has left her short on tour guides inside the house. James and I will cover the music and dining rooms." She scrunched her face and eyed Robert and Jane. "She asked me to see if you two would take the library. Rita will provide the costumes."

"If she doesn't lace me up so tight in that corset, I'd love to." Jane turned to Robert. "Are you willing?"

Robert grimaced but held his hands palms out. "I'll try it."

Jane clapped her hands. "The library is my favorite room in the house. It will be fun."

Robert puffed out his cheeks. "Playing dress up has never made it on my fun list."

Cameo laughed. "You will make a stellar 1800s man." She turned to her mother. "Mom, you know you have a standing invitation to participate."

Katherine held up her hand. "Thanks, but the place gives me a headache."

Cameo sighed. "I know. I thought ... maybe ..."

"I'll be outside with the carolers and the children's Christmas play," Katherine said. "When you complete your duties with the house tour, join me."

Strange. Katherine was so negative, even combatant and resentful when it came to the Topazus mansion, but she had a love for the outside activities and the land itself. Cameo displayed mismatched emotions regarding her mother. On one hand their relationship was strained due to the legal trust, yet they each respected the other's talents and abilities.

Their arrangement mirrored Jane's relationship with her brother. The surface was friendly, but hiding underneath was frustration.

CHAPTER SIX

Jane's blue taffeta skirt rustled as she entered the library to find Robert, eyes closed, resting his head on a wing-back chair with his legs outstretched.

"You look relaxed."

Robert opened one eye. Then sat up abruptly. "You look ... nice ... your hair parted in the middle and all."

"Are you making fun?"

"No." He sent her a pained look and straightened his ascot and red brocade vest.

Her breath caught, corset withstanding. Robert's dark hair and neatly trimmed stubble beard made for a dashing gentleman of the 1800s. For an instant she saw him as a guy. As in a guy she'd like to look nice for. But he was just a friend who happened to be a guy ... and her employer.

"Well, I thank you for the compliment." Jane patted her hair. "Rita is an expert in antebellum dress. She anchored my hair with a hairpiece. These were called rats." She turned her head and pointed to the nape of her neck. "It's a small net stuffed with hair gathered from hair brushing."

"I hope it's a rat that doesn't run the walls at night."

"Sheesh, me too." She dangled a tiny drawstring purse hanging from her wrist in front of her. "Look at this dinky thing. A wallet wouldn't even fit in here."

"Back in the day, if you showed up as a guest with the purse you carry, they'd have thought you were moving in."

She huffed a sigh. "I would have been an oddity. Rita said these tiny purses might hold a handkerchief, coins, or gloves. I've got way more stuff than that."

Robert tugged at his collar. "Rita gave me a choice of a string tie or this thing. I thought the ascot might be more comfortable, but I was wrong. Comfort was apparently unknown to people of the nineteenth century." He pushed out of the chair. "I could have made a bundle as a recliner salesman. What happened to the computer in here?"

"Rita put it away, not wanting to detract from authentic 1800s look."

"Makes sense."

James with Cameo on his arm walked in the library. They made a handsome couple.

"I hear Mother commandeered you two," James said. He wore a loose-fitting woolen suit jacket with a vest, a white shirt with a high starched collar and a bow tie. Cameo wore a gold-colored hooped dress that accented her chestnut hair parted in the middle with curly ringlets bouncing on the sides.

"Have you learned your parts yet?" Cameo asked.

"She has." Robert nodded toward Jane. "I plan to

be a non-speaking prop."

"What if someone asks you a question?" Jane asked.

"I shall refer them to you."

"Smart man," James said.

Cameo stretched out her hand. "Robert, let me see your phone."

Robert complied. She swiped the screen and tapped on the phone's keyboard. "I'll pull up a YouTube presentation given by Rita before a bridesmaid luncheon this past summer. Here … watch this video and you'll have an idea of the information she'll present to visitors before you see them tonight." She plopped the phone back in Robert's hand.

Cameo was good at issuing orders.

"Yes, ma'am." He saluted her.

Jane smiled inside. Robert may not be thrilled about dressing up, but he was a good sport.

In the video, Rita wore a blue and white patterned gown with puffy lace-trimmed sleeves, delicate dangling earrings, elbow-length gloves, and the topaz ring. She appeared stately and poised.

"She puts on a realistic show," Robert said.

"I know. I watched her at the tea this morning. It's as though she morphs into Martha Lee."

On the video, Rita shared Topazus history and when she showed the participants the elliptical fan window over the front door, a ray of light touched the ring, sparking an extra red radiance. She held her gloved hand up as she had done when Jane saw her in the dressing room. Jane's eyes remained glued on the ring in the video as she pointed out the windows and doors designed to line up for cross ventilation.

Rita in the flesh stepped into the library. "Our guests will arrive shortly. Take your places and we shall welcome them."

"She takes this play-acting seriously," Jane whispered.

Robert closed out the video, and they moved to the library doorway where Rita's instructions to James and Cameo could be heard

"Mary Sue has prepared hors d'oeuvres. Arranged on the buffet in the dining room, you'll see assorted cheeses, crackers and cookies. James, you discourage any overindulgence. Cameo, explain the music room's furnishings and please don't allow anyone to play the harpsichord. I do not want it damaged." She adjusted her gloves and wiggled her ring finger.

"Do you notice something about that ring compared to the one in the video?" Jane asked Robert.

"She has a habit of lifting her finger and brandishing the ring."

"Yes. But the ring itself. The one on the video was decidedly deeper in color."

"It could be the lighting or just the way it looks on the video."

"But still ... I think the one in the video was the real thing."

Robert frowned and opened the video again. This video was posted on May 19, 2019.

"Wasn't the ring theft payoff the year before?" Jane asked. "If that ring is genuine ..."

Robert dropped the phone back in his pocket. "Something is out of whack."

~

With electric lights turned off, the flickering

candlelight in the hall and the lantern lights in the rooms should have set the mood for an authentic 1800s evening, but for Robert they cast shadows of mystery on the house and those who held a stake in it.

"I wish we'd had these candles and lanterns last night when the lights went out," Jane said.

"Especially if they shed light on who sneaked in and stole the computer drive."

The front door opened, and a Beau stepped in with a group of spectators clustered behind him. "Guests are here." Rita glided down the hall toward the drawing room. "Smiles everyone."

Robert followed Jane back into the library.

"Genetics," Jane said.

"What's that?"

"Genetics may account for Cameo's bossy attitude. If Rita's depiction of Martha Lee is spot on, Cameo may have inherited her grandmother's dictatorial attitude."

"You got a point. Her instructions resemble Cameo's when she lays out work in her office."

"I think we're on to something. Rita provided me with a summary sheet for library tour guides and directed me to memorize it," Jane said.

"Which I know you gladly did." He'd never worked with anyone like Jane, keen on history and following orders. That was not the norm for investigators. "All the more reason for me to send any inquiries to you, teammate."

"Team implies you have a job. Mind telling me what it is?"

He wiggled his brows, shoved his index finger under his collar and pulled. "My part is wearing this ensemble."

He was rewarded with a bump to the shoulder.

"Listen up." She read from the instruction sheet. "Twelve people are allowed in at a time for the tour. Rita gathers them for the overall lecture about the history of Topazus in the drawing room. Then the guests can explore the downstairs rooms and ask questions. That's when we play the parts of Martha Lee's cousin and her husband visiting from Boston."

"Good. I'll play the know-nothing husband of the know-it-all cousin that does all the talking."

Jane shook her head slowly in I-give-up fashion, placed the instruction sheet in the desk drawer and went to explore more of the book titles. Robert approached the fireplace wall surrounded by musty books. He ran his fingers along the mantle and down the sides to the stone hearth but couldn't find anything that might conceal a trigger to open a secret entrance. "Where did your brother find the hidden door in the dining room?"

"The door blended in with the wallpaper, making it invisible. The release button was behind a fire brick with no mortar," Jane said.

Robert examined the fire bricks, running his hand across the rough surface and peering into the opening.

"Mister, are you looking for Santa?"

Robert raised up, jarring his head. Rubbing the bump, he said, "We Victorians don't believe in Santa Claus."

"Johnny? There you are," a woman said. "Do not wander off."

"That man says there's no Santa Claus."

"What?" She scowled. "Why tell the child that?"

"I ... I'm ..."

"Don't mind him." Jane swooped in. "He's just my husband."

Just?

With a flick of the wrist, she took command. "We're from Boston and in our area, people view Christmas in a variety of ways." She took Johnny by the hand. "Come, let me show you an old photo of Santa. Some people refer to him as St. Nick."

Johnny's mother gave Robert a sideways glare and followed behind Jane.

Robert returned to his exploration, but a man and woman wandered in and then another couple with small children followed. Thankfully, Jane motioned to the couple with children. The woman studied book titles near the fireplace and promptly sneezed. Robert steered clear of the Santa controversy and addressed the man. What might a fellow from Boston talk about in the 1800s? He'd try weather.

"My wife and I arrived a few days ago from Boston." Robert leaned casually against the desk. "We're glad to be below the Mason-Dixon line, avoiding the snow."

The man's brows scrunched together. "Isn't that a racial statement? I wouldn't think it proper to separate the North and South like that." Robert should have stuck to his original plan and let Jane do all the talking.

"I ... uh ... don't quite know how to answer that, sir."

His wife joined them "I'd like to explore more of the library, but my eyes are watering." She pulled out a handkerchief and blew her nose. "I hope I'm not coming down with a cold. I want to enjoy the holidays."

"Ma'am. The hot mulled cider in the dining room

across the hall might take the edge off the chill."
Sending them on their way might be a way out of his
predicament.

"Why thank you. Hot cider sounds good." She
headed toward the dining room but left her husband
behind.

The man leaned in and lowered his voice. "Any
word on the guy that was murdered?"

"A murder in these parts? Sometimes news is slow
to reach us."

The man chuckled. "You're pretty good at playing
your part. If you're really not from here, you may not
know the girl serving in the dining room used to work
in Leo Calhoun's house."

"And who's Leo Calhoun?"

"State senator." He dropped the name with flair.
"My wife is friends with his wife. The murder victim,
Alfred Berdanier was Leo's attorney, and we frequently
dined with him at Leo's. Mary Sue served us," he tilted
his head down and peered at Robert over his glasses,
"until she had to be let go. Interesting coincidence her
being here." He wrinkled his forehead, looking for a
reaction from Robert.

Robert shrugged in his cousin-from-Boston role.
But the investigator inside him stirred. The triangular
connection of Mary Sue, the state senator and Berdanier
may mean nothing, yet it was an unusual fact. Was
there more to her working at Topazus than coincidence?

"Horace?" His wife stuck head back in the room.
"Coming?"

He flinched but whispered one last piece of gossip.
"Mary Sue was made to leave. And it was sudden." He
gave Robert a you-know-what-I-mean wink. Only

Robert had no clue what he meant. "Yes, dear," he called to his wife and left the room.

A fresh set of curious eyes on a young girl of perhaps twelve or thirteen entered the library. She wore a knit cap pulled snug over her ears. A man accompanied her, perhaps her father. His eyes darted from the girl to Robert, Jane, and then back to the girl. His gait declared a determination to move through the tour as quickly as possible.

"Did you know there was a murder here?" the girl asked. Her eyes roamed the room as if a body might still be lying around.

"I did hear that."

"Kendall. That's an inappropriate question and none of our concern."

"But Daddy, you talked about it all the way over here."

The girl stated simple childlike truth. Adults were prone to whitewash feelings. Like the man preceding the young girl who didn't have the courage to share openly. He disguised his words with provocative gestures and secretive hints instead.

"I keep up with the local news," the man with the young girl admitted.

The visitors' curiosity about Berdanier's death did not surprise Robert. People often claim to want good news and complain about the bad, yet no one fails to note murder.

"Perhaps you would be interested in joining my wife who is sharing tales of Christmas and its customs," Robert said to the youngster.

The father and child joined Jane's presentation and Robert moved closer to listen.

"The gift-giving by Saint Nicholas lives on in our Christmas traditions today." She held up a storybook. "These stories and many more are the wonderful legacy given in books like those preserved in the Topazus library." She gestured about the room then pointed to the door. "Enjoy seasonal treats in the dining room across the hall. Thank you for coming."

She was a natural. He could picture Jane's kindergarten students hanging on her every word. After the last of the guests filtered through, Rita came in pulling off her gloves. Since Jane made such an issue of the ring, Robert took special notice. The ring she wore was a deep pink gem in a setting of clear stones—decidedly not as brilliant as the one on the video.

~

Outside, the Yule log burned in the bonfire. Robert saw Katherine seated in the pavilion on the other side of the fire. She waved Robert and Jane over. "I see you dressed for Rita."

Robert pulled at his ascot. "I don't know how men stood these stiff collars."

"Makes you look dignified." Jane said.

"And you looked magnified, like ten times the hip size."

Jane cocked a brow. "Never know what's hidden underneath."

"Ah ... you have spoken truth," Katherine said. Those skirts could hide a multitude of ills. But it looks like we've traded one means of hiding with another." She nodded toward two teenagers sitting by the bonfire with their faces concealed behind electronic devices.

"Interesting observation," Robert said. Besides the preoccupied teens gathered around the fire, James,

Cameo and Rita formed a chat group and Micah stood opposite them in the flickering shadows of the blaze. While Jane talked to Katherine, Robert excused himself and joined Micah on the far side of the bonfire.

"The embers look perfect for roasting marshmallows," Robert said.

"Or hot dogs." Micah nodded toward two children roasting skewered wieners. "We have a vendor who offers both."

"Fun for kids. Do you have children?"

"Two. Fourteen and fifteen. They think they're too old for all this."

Robert nodded. "They think they're ready to break free?"

"Just like that fire." The light from the flames reflected in his eyes.

"I don't have children of my own, but as a lawman I've witnessed the desire of teens to be their own person. Break free. Be on their own. But left to their own devices, many burn bridges and then discover their road to freedom is not free after all. There are consequences."

They stood and watched the crackling of the fire for a while, the heat penetrating.

"What about you?" Robert asked. Any regrets of not breaking free of Topazus?"

"Working the land ... it's all I know ... all I ever cared about. I was born into it. But now with the controversy…"

Micah shoved his hands in his pockets and lifted his eyes to meet Robert's. He seemed to inaudibly ask, "Should I say what I'm really thinking?"

But his eyes dropped. The moment died away as a

leaf caught fire, shriveled and dissolved into a puff of smoke.

"Robert," Jane called to him, "the play is about to start."

"You go ahead. I have to keep an eye on the fire."

With that statement Micah gave him one long hard stare and then returned his focus on the fire. The fire played with shadows across his face. His stare searing, disquieting Robert's heart.

The Christmas play was a cute presentation by a children's group teaching Santa Claus about the birth of Jesus. At the end of the play voices of the group, which now included Dean and Mary Sue, united in singing *Hark the Herald Angels Sing*. But as he fingered his ascot, Robert's investigator intuition told him the gathering of amiable participants also contained a clever thief, and potentially a killer.

CHAPTER SEVEN

Sunday morning lifted Jane's spirits. The ten-minute walk with Robert along the road covered with a canopy of oaks led them to the Topazus church.

She stood back to take in the full view of the white clapboard chapel with a bell tower steeple.

Robert pointed. "There's a plaque over there."

"Ah." Jane shot him a grin. He understood her penchant for historic markers. She stepped to the building and read the inscription: *Topazus Chapel erected in 1865 in thanks for the ending of the Civil War and as a memorial to all the men who fought and died on both sides.*

Inside the chapel, Jane picked up a brochure and took a seat on a pew with Robert near the middle of the church. The quaint, one-room sanctuary held ten pews stretching the width of the building, with side aisles and a small platform with a podium up front.

The brochure told the story of the twin Clark brothers who became soldiers in the Civil War—Davis-

Confederate, Daniel-Union. When the war ended, only Daniel returned. The chapel became a place of prayer for the safe return of Davis and other soldiers. After nine months, on Christmas Eve, 1865, Davis returned, and the brothers reunited beside the cedar tree still standing outside the chapel.

Jane ran her fingers over the photo of the Reconciliation Tree and stopped at the quote underneath: *Conflicts end when people change.*

She set down the brochure, thinking of the tree standing outside that had witnessed the reunion of brothers who fought on opposite sides of the Civil War. The burning sensation of tears threatened. She had reconnected with her brother. But reconciliation, how did that happen? For two so diametrically opposed, what changes did the twin brothers make? What changes did her brother and she have to make?

She silently prayed. *Lord, give me a heart to forgive, as these brothers did. Remove the resentment toward my brother that gnaws at me. Somehow help us to reconcile.*

She studied the roughhewn cross that hung in the front of the church. Her attitude toward Adam had not been charitable since he failed to come and see their mother before she died. Graveside, Jane had confronted him.

"Why did you bother coming now?" Jane had seethed. "Mother's dead. Gone. Can no longer see you." Jane's insides burned like fire. "I had to lie to her, tell her you were on your way. I begged her to hold on." Tears, dripping off Jane's face, angered her more. She poked Adam in the chest. "Were you waiting for her to die?" Those who had come to the graveyard retreated to their cars. Decorum didn't enter Jane's mind. Adam stared at her. Just stood and said nothing. Fuming, Jane hurled her final words, "I'll never forgive you for making me lie to her."

It had been six months since she swore her unforgiveness and stormed away. Yet Adam came yesterday. Was reconciliation possible?

She could relate to Cameo and Katherine's strained relationship, being at odds over Topazus. Seating in the chapel reflected their division. Katherine sat in a pew near the front with Dean. Rita, James, and Cameo filed in the row behind Robert and Jane. Could the cedar tree beside the church that stood as a peacemaking icon be witness to their reconciliation as it had for their ancestors?

Bed-and-breakfast guests, Horace and Thelma Baxter who had come to the historical tour last night also took seats on the pew behind them.

Micah, his family and other visitors continued filing in until the church was filled.

A young man who appeared all of sixteen but must have been old enough to attend college stepped to the podium.

"Good morning." His voiced cracked.

The congregation muttered good mornings in return.

He cleared his throat and began again. "I am Dennis Wellborn from Low Country Bible College." He swallowed hard. "Shall we open in pra ... prayer?" He prayed and Jane said her own silent prayer for a peace to settle over the young preacher.

Katherine quietly stepped to the platform and placed a bottle of water beside him.

"Sorry, but no need to tell you I am nervous. You poor folks in God's mysterious providence have been selected to hear my first try at presenting a sermon." He unscrewed the bottle cap and took a swallow. Dean spoke up and said, "We're ready to hear whatever you have to say."

"Thank you." He squeezed his eyes closed but when he reopened them, he grabbed hold of the sides of the podium and gave a message that spoke to Jane's heart.

"I am attempting to appear as a person holding enough knowledge to warrant commanding your attention. But that is a mask. A cover-up. A disguise. Because underneath is a scared little boy who has pored over scripture in hopes of latching onto God's power to present a meaningful message. And to speak it without fainting dead away." He looked up.

"Don't be scared of us. Preach it." Horace bellowed.

A smile and a laugh cut through his tension. He took another swig of water and launched into his sermon.

He spoke of the tendency we have to wear invisible masks and pretend to be something we are not.

"But what harm is there in pretending?"

The question struck Jane. She wore two masks. One tried to cover resentment, the other covered the longing inside to reconnect with her brother.

"Masks," Wellborn said, "prevent us from the relationships we could have. Hiding feelings empowers the negative things we hold inside. To maximize the lives God wants for us, we must take a risky step, take off our masks and be honest."

He was talking directly to her.

After a closing prayer. Jane wiped her tear-filled eyes, masking her desire to weep. The sermon landed hard on the negative thoughts she held in secret toward her brother. And she wasn't the only one in the room attempting to camouflage tears.

Robert took out his handkerchief, blew his nose, and gave her a sheepish grin. "His remarks struck like an arrow to the heart."

Jane gave him an understanding nod. Though vindicated, Robert still struggled to cover the hurt resulting from accusations that had been made against him when he worked for ABI. The result was his early retirement from law enforcement.

Two children are headed your way," Robert said.

Jane saw Adam first and her heart leapt. She hurried to him. "You came and brought Bradley and Nathan." She gave the six- and seven-year-old boys hugs. "Where's Bethany?"

"She had an altar guild meeting this afternoon, but the boys wanted to come."

"And you didn't?"

"Well ... me too. It's not often we're able to see each other."

Masks in place, an invisible wall remained. But maybe scaling the wall was possible if they took it slow.

After introductions, they enjoyed sampling the homemade soups volunteers brought to the pavilion as a fundraiser for the Bible college.

Katherine announced the afternoon children's games. Bradley and Nathan hurried to join in.

Rita took the mic. "Adults. We're not leaving you

out. There will be activities inside the house followed by coffee, tea or mulled cider—your choice."

In the music room, all the bed-and-breakfast guests plus Adam took seats in folding chairs arranged in a circle.

A Belle, Sydney, gave instructions. "Our game is Fact or Fib. Each of you tell two crazy Christmas presents you have received; one must be true, the other a lie. The rest guess which is the lie."

After a few minutes, Sydney said, "If everyone is ready, do we have a volunteer to go first?"

"I'll go." Horace shimmied to the edge of his seat. "One Christmas I received a lump of coal in my stocking and cried." He made a pitiful face. "Another time, I received a really heavy box. I said it felt like it must be a rock. And it was! Which is the lie?" Everyone took turns guessing and were evenly split with their answers.

"So, tell us. Who is right?" Sydney asked.

"It was the rock. And the rock turned out to be a fine specimen of granite and a business for me." He settled back in his chair. Thelma patted his knee.

Jane's contribution was a gift of a parakeet or a box of bubble wrap for stress relief. Adam knew which of her stories was true. He'd given her the parakeet. When all was said and done the best fib voted by all came from Thelma, Horace's wife. She claimed her craziest gift was a box of nothing because she had told family members, "Please don't get me anything."

She was being awarded her ribbon when Cameo excused herself to take a phone call. In minutes she returned and tapped James on the shoulder. She whispered to him, and the jovial expression dropped from his face. Cameo pointed at Robert and motioned for Jane to come as well. They met in the hall. Concern etched Cameo's face.

"Mother was arrested for Berdanier's murder."

~

Robert watched as the unmarked black sedan carrying Katherine, moved slowly behind the cheering children running the candy cane relay. The scene produced a contrast in gaiety and gravity.

Cameo hurried past him, digging in her purse. "They're booking Mom at the sheriff's office and I'm going." James hurried alongside her, taking the keys from Cameo's hand. "I'll drive you."

"Keep me posted," Robert said. Cameo raised her hand to Robert and kept moving.

"What do we do now?" Jane asked.

"The best thing we can do is help keep things on an even keel until five o'clock when the afternoon events are over." He checked his watch. Thirty minutes. "Spend time with your brother and nephews and I'm going to help Micah in the pavilion. Then meet me in the library."

Helping stack chairs on a cart, Robert asked Micah, "What are your thoughts on Katherine's arrest?"

"Katherine was upset with Berdanier." He folded the legs on a table with a smack. "But saying Katherine snuck off and shot Berdanier ..." he shook his head "... no way. I saw her on the trail behind Crest Manor after the luncheon."

"Did you tell that to the investigator?"

"Yes. After the luncheon I came out here to change burned out fluorescent light bulbs and saw her."

Robert looked at the light fixture that did not work

when he flipped the switch earlier. If he just changed the bulbs, why wasn't it working?

Micah must have noticed his questioning glance. He shoved the folded table against the others with a *bang*. "New bulbs didn't work on all these lights. Some need new ballasts."

Robert returned to the point that could be significant in helping Katherine. "Seeing Katherine on the river trail after the luncheon, I believe is important. For her to have shot Berdanier, she wouldn't have had time to take the long walk down to the river and then go to the front gate. Are you sure it was her?"

Micah motioned to Robert to stand next to him. "If you stand right here and look up, that is the back of Crest Manor. The trail extends to the left on the ridge of the hill. I could see Katherine, at least I believe it was her, since she said she went for a walk to the river."

"Could you make out anything specific?"

Micah shrugged, "The person had on a light-colored top."

~

Robert opened the rear door to the main hall, thankful to get out of the chilling wind, and made a mental note to ask Jane if she remembered what everyone was wearing at lunch. The evidence might be there to arrest Katherine Clark for the murder of Alfred Berdanier, but Robert had that twinge of doubt—an inkling hard to define—that told him she didn't do it.

And if she didn't shoot Berdanier, someone else did. First look at the obvious. But if the obvious isn't correct, you look to the plausible. The theory of the shot coming from a careless hunter did not fit because of the gun caliber.

Robert waited for Jane in the hall in front of a seven-foot-high painting of a garden. Lori, his wife who died, would have enjoyed tackling that art project. She loved flowers and had the talent to capture them on canvas. The rear door opened, breaking the memory.

"Whew." Jane stamped her feet against the doormat and rubbed her arms covered with only a light-weight sweater. It gets cold when the sun goes down, and it's a damp chill. "My brother and another carload were the last to leave the property. Micah closed the gates behind them."

"Did you have a good visit with your brother?"

"Cordial."

"I hope it's a step in the right direction for you both."

She took in a deep breath and released a short blast of tense air. "Me too. I'm still having trouble getting past how he treated mother."

"At least you've made a start. Family rifts need to be healed. And that's what we are apparently in the midst of here at Topazus."

"What's the latest on Katherine's arrest?"

"Cameo texted that she is on her way from the Bennett County Sheriff's Office where they're holding Katherine. She'll meet us here."

Jane shook her head. "I cannot fathom Katherine shooting Berdanier."

"Since she has no qualms about handling a rifle, it won't help her case."

"Yes. But shooting pests is different."

"Some would say Berdanier was a pest."

"You think she did it?"

"I'm not saying that. What we must consider is the

fact that she could have shot him. She had the gun, marksmanship and motive."

"Did she confess?"

"If she was wise, she said nothing. With a criminal attorney for a daughter, she should know to only say that she wants a lawyer."

"But doesn't that make her seem guilty? On television when a suspect says they want a lawyer, they're usually the guilty party."

"We haven't reached the climax of this story and we have to look at things from the defense's point of view, not the prosecution. Come in the library and have a seat. I'll teach you the facts of investigative life."

Jane unhooked her large handbag from her shoulder and pulled out her notepad. "Are rules forthcoming?"

"You've got it." Jane was efficient in keeping track of rules which were nothing more than basic law enforcement principles he had acquired over the years. Textbooks had their place, but there was nothing like learning on the job.

Jane sneezed as she entered the room, pulled a tissue from her bag and sneezed again.

"I believe these musty old books that I love make me sneeze. The damp air seems to make it worse." She plunked down on a leather wing-back chair and placed the notepad on her lap.

Robert sat at the writing desk and turned on the lamp. "Here's a rule to add to your others. What number are we on?"

"Number seven. Six was the one about having a backup in tenuous situations."

"Okay. Number seven. Criminal prosecution and

defense see a case from opposite points of view. Here's why. The prosecution tries to prove the guilt of an identified suspect; the defense takes an identified suspect and tries to establish reasonable doubt about his guilt."

Robert folded his arms, pressing against the desk. "As a lawman, I've been accustomed to working from the prosecutor's point of view. My job was to deliver a detailed case to support probable cause for a person's arrest. Now, helping the defense, I must shift gears and look at a case from the point of view of the accused."

"Like the case we just worked with Sheriff Barnes in Pine County?"

"Exactly. And having been in the shoes of a defendant myself, it is not pleasant. For the accused, it is like falling into a frozen lake at a weak spot and then hoping he or she can find a place to get back out. The people above the lake have all the equipment and plenty of air, while the one underneath has limited time and resources."

"Makes sense for defendants to have an attorney provided if they can't afford one. What happens now to Katherine?"

"Cameo said that bond was not recommended, which is usual with a murder charge. She'll be held in jail until first appearance."

"Is that when she pleads guilty or not guilty?"

"No. First appearance is like judicial house-keeping making certain everything is neat and tidy in terms of the arrest. The court wants to ensure that there is a sufficient basis to hold the defendant in jail and reexamine the bond that has been set. The judge also makes sure the defendant was not pressured improperly to waive his rights, informs him or her of the exact charges and reminds the person that he or she has the right to an attorney."

"Even though they are at odds over the property, Cameo seems to be coming to her mother's defense."

"No matter how strained the relationship, Cameo would not want her mother accused of murder. Do you remember what color everyone was wearing at the luncheon on Friday?"

Jane started to write then jerked up her head. "Is this a test?"

"A test of your observation and memory. Excellent practice and it may have a bearing on the case."

"Hmm." Jane closed her eyes. "I have to picture the table and where everyone was seated. Let's see. I know Berdanier had on a red and green plaid sweater vest. Cameo was wearing a cream-colored cashmere jacket over a brown turtleneck, James had on a brown tweed jacket, Rita a white sweater, Micah a gray jacket and blue or blue-gray shirt, Katherine a light pink wool jacket over a white blouse. Dean had on a black sport coat."

Robert stared as she rattled off the clothing and colors. He remembered some of what she described but would have been hard pressed to recall what everyone wore. "You pass recall. And it sounds like all the women had on light-colored tops. Micah said he saw someone in a light-colored top on the path behind Crest Manor after the luncheon and believes it was Katherine. But it could have been Katherine, Rita or Cameo he saw behind the manor."

"Cameo and Katherine said they went to Crest Manor, and Rita—who knows?" Jane said. "And what would be Katherine's motive for killing Berdanier anyhow?"

"Anything Berdanier pursued that hurt the sale to the developer disturbed Katherine."

"Kill him if he blocks the sale that Cameo wasn't likely to approve anyhow?" Jane shook her head.

"She may have felt Cameo would consider the sale because of the financial problems the estate is facing." Robert said.

"If you ask who benefits from his death, what about Cameo?" Jane asked. "With Berdanier out of the picture, control of the estate passes to her."

"A valid point. On the side of selling, would be Katherine and Dean. On the side of hanging on to the property would be Rita, James, Cameo and probably Micah. Unclear to me, was where Berdanier stood."

Robert pushed back from the desk and walked to the shelves next to the fireplace. "In Rita's case, she felt it necessary to obtain a clean report on mold and mildew." Robert pulled a book off the shelf and ran his finger against the cover. "These books have a thin dusting of mildew. Why the cover up?"

"The mildew is probably what is making me sneeze."

"Yes. Thelma sneezed when she walked in the room last night." Robert brushed the residue from his fingers.

"If there were costly repairs and they knew the estate was in a financial bind ..." Jane began.

Robert finished. "It was easier to keep the problems covered up." He slapped the top of the mantle and a carved section of trim shot out. He stared at it. "Well ... well ..." Robert peered inside. His pulse quickened.

Jane hurried over. "Anything in it?"

"There certainly is."

Jane stood on tiptoes to see inside the little drawer and whispered. "The missing drive."

CHAPTER EIGHT

"Remember the scraping noise when the lights went out?" Robert asked. "It could have been the drawer sliding out."

"What about the sneeze and someone stepping on my foot? You need to keep looking for a concealed entrance into the library. Someone wanted the drive hidden, but who?" Jane asked.

"Fingerprints may tell us." Robert pulled a clean handkerchief from his pocket and carefully removed the drive.

"Can you lift fingerprints?"

"No. But my ABI buddy, Vance, can have it done. Do you have a tissue in your purse?"

Jane handed one to him. Robert crumpled the tissue and carefully nested the drive on it. "If there are prints, I don't want to smear them."

A rumbling sound came from across the hall.

"Quick. Place this in your purse and try not to jostle it. Don't mention finding the drive or the drawer.

That includes Cameo." Robert pushed the drawer back in place and propped his arm on the mantle while Jane returned to her seat.

Rita appeared in the doorway with a tea cart brimming with delectable goodies, a teapot, coffee pot, napkins and Styrofoam cups. "James texted and asked me to join you and relayed a message from Cameo. Robert, she wants you to get her briefcase from her car. I hope you don't mind disposable cups. Mary Sue is cleaning up and these are some goodies left from the buffet."

"Disposable cups and leftovers are welcome," Robert said.

"They should be here shortly and I'm still finishing in the kitchen. In the meantime, enjoy." Rita placed the tray on the narrow library table behind a settee and left the room.

Robert pointed at the cups. "Disposable is perfect for us to obtain fingerprints, if we can retrieve the cups after they're used without smudging the prints."

"Whose prints do you want?"

"Everyone's. Watch who handles what." It was a long shot but gathering prints from Rita, James and Cameo might help identify or rule out who handled the drive. What was strange is the drive was still hidden. He could understand hiding it to keep from being caught with it. But it seemed whoever took it, would have removed it before now. Unless they didn't have the opportunity without being seen. "Get ready for rule number eight."

"I'll have to remember this one, I don't want to disturb you know what nesting in my purse," Jane whispered.

"Everyone is a suspect until they're not a suspect."

"Even Cameo?"

He gave an emphatic nod. "I'd better go get Cameo's briefcase."

"Do you have a key to her car?"

"No. But I know her keyless entry code. I'll be right back while you bask in the joy of all the historical wonders in this library."

Cameo's car was parked behind the bed-and-breakfast. He found her case on the floorboard behind the driver's seat. The title of a document on the back seat caught his eye: *Can You Trust Your Trustee?*

He picked up the paper and saw that she had highlighted a subheading: *Trustees and Mismanagement.* Was Cameo concerned enough about Berdanier's handling of the trust to remove him, as in permanently?

He placed the paper back on the seat, grabbed the briefcase, and returned to the house. Jane was standing by the fireplace. She held up a book and started to speak when tires screeched to a stop on the brick drive out front. Robert turned and stepped back into the hall. In a moment, James entered, shaking his head. Cameo was behind him. Her heels clicked against the wood floor in a hurried cadence.

"Cameo drove?" Robert asked.

"Remind me to never let her drive again. Will you?"

Robert chuckled and slapped him on the shoulder. "You won't need a reminder."

"I heard that." "Like you gentlemen never speed. I keep it reasonable."

James rolled his eyes toward Robert. "Reasonably

close to supersonic."

Cameo breezed past them, leaving the faint scent of cologne in her wake. "Let's get on to more important matters."

In the library, Cameo persisted. "Men," she directed the word to Jane. "It's okay for them to speed, but they somehow freak if a woman does. Double standard, wouldn't you say?"

Rita re-entered. "Jane, I would give the answer lawyers always advise. No comment."

Jane smiled and shelved the book she held in her hand.

"Rita, you have snacks for us. Thank you," Cameo said.

"Nothing elegant."

"I don't need elegant, just edible," James said. "The soup I had for lunch is long gone."

Everyone fixed small plates of marmalade-filled tear drop cookies, shortbread, roasted pecans and tiny ham and cucumber sandwiches. They sat in a semi-circle. Cameo and James in wing-back chairs faced Rita on a side chair and Robert and Jane on the settee.

Robert kept track of where each person set down their Styrofoam cups.

"Were you able to talk to your mother?" Rita asked Cameo.

"Yes. But seeing her in the orange jail jumpsuit ..." Cameo choked on the words, "...was a jolt. I wasn't prepared for it."

James reached over to squeeze her hand. "Understandable. That's why I called Pruitt."

"Good," Rita said.

James turned to Robert and Jane. "Pruitt Jennings

handles most of the criminal cases in our law firm. He will be at first appearance with the judge in the morning. Agent Kelley told him that the Circuit Solicitor's Office had the complaint and would likely file information tomorrow afternoon. At that time, we'll be able to see what they have."

For twenty-five years, Robert had worked with the prosecution. Explaining the prosecutor's objective as opposed to the defense to Jane was easy. However, shifting sides unsettled him, like he was a defector. But the important factor remained: to find the truth behind Berdanier's murder, wherever that pursuit led.

Cameo clasped her hands. "I wish I could represent Mom ... or you could, James,"

"We would make great partners in Katherine's defense, but it's not advisable to represent a family member or a family friend," James said.

"This is all just too crazy." Cameo forced her fingers through her thick hair. "I know Mom had no love lost for Berdanier. And he rubbed people the wrong way, but ..."

"He stirred things and enjoyed upsetting people," James said.

Rita grasped the arms of her chair and pushed to her feet. "He tried to make a big deal about mildew." She jerked her head toward Jane. "I know your brother found a problem in the dining room, but it must be isolated. Brandon, who checked the house, is a reputable young man. I did not appreciate Berdanier's snide attitude regarding the report. I paid for it myself."

Cameo stood and paced. "Whatever mold or mildew was found we must clean, so it doesn't get worse. Jane, can you check with your brother about a cleaning service?"

Rita jerked her head toward Cameo. "But I—"

Cameo stopped pacing and turned to Rita. "You are too kind. I don't want you footing the bill. We'll reimburse you for the report and have the mildew cleaned."

"Another thing I'm interested in is Chandler Development." Cameo clicked open the locks on her briefcase that Robert had placed on the desk. "I have the information from their website and the company corporation financials that Robert obtained. Since Dean is their local representative, is there anything else you know about the company?" She directed the question to Rita and James.

"They want to build condos." Rita sniffed and sat back down. "I fear Topazus and the entire property will change forever. All the traditions we've struggled to keep alive over the years—gone."

Robert went on a fishing expedition. "We have a mystery to solve."

"Oh?" Cameo turned to Robert, a puzzled look on her face.

James face scrunched into a thoughtful pose.

"Mystery? I love a mystery," Rita said.

Robert delivered the scenario, ready to take in the reactions. "It's a mystery that occurred right under our noses in this very room. A computer drive was being viewed by Cameo, Jane, and myself when the power went out. Cameo left the room to find the fuse box. James arrived in the dark and helped get the lights back on. Jane and I remained in this room. When the lights came back on, the drive was gone. What do you suppose happened to the drive?"

Rita pressed her hands against her knees and kneaded them. "And you say this really happened?"

James took a sip of his coffee and nodded. "The house was dark when I arrived. Not an unusual occurrence around here."

Cameo, still holding the papers she'd taken from her briefcase, appeared to glance toward the fireplace, then pushed the briefcase closed with a *thud*. "Yes. Jane found a thumb drive at Berdanier's office. We were looking at the content files when the power went off."

"And the mystery is that when the lights came back on the drive was gone. Theories anyone?" Robert cast the question—a fisherman trying his luck.

"This was the night of the murder?" Rita asked.

"Yes," Jane said. "We returned from Berdanier's office. You were here, Rita, preparing for the children's tea the next day."

"And I brought you tea and then left to go to the store. So, who ... Katherine was at the manor and Micah I think was still around dealing with Christmas lights. He'd said something about extension cords."

"Jane or Robert would be first on my list of suspects." James said, a smirk on his face.

"James." Rita admonished her son.

"It's okay," Robert said. "I was just telling Jane; everyone is a suspect until they are not a suspect."

"There's a thought-provoking statement," Cameo said. "It could have been any of us who took the drive."

"I certainly don't care what Berdanier had on his old drive," Rita said. "Besides, police have completed their investigation and released access to his office records. Why take the drive?"

"The thumb drive was taken before the police

cleared access to Berdanier's office," Robert said.

"Someone feared information that might be on there." James bit into a cookie and brushed crumbs off his pant leg.

"Well, I don't know if Katherine shot him, but whoever did, did us a favor," Rita said and folded her arms in front of her. "He was always playing us—pushing buttons."

"Bringing up the heir's property angered Katherine," James said.

Jane spoke up. "I suppose Dean would be out a big commission if the property sale was nixed with potential heirs' property claims?"

"And I wonder about Micah. Would he be forced out, if developers moved in?" Robert asked.

"While you're naming suspects, there's always me." Rita stood, pointing both index fingers to herself. "I might lose my catering business. And of course," she pointed at James, "you might lose the role of playing Daniel."

Cameo held up her hands. "All right. With Berdanier dead, I gain control of the property. Let's face it, we all had our qualms about Berdanier, and we could sit here and speculate all night. But it has been a long day. James and I must be at the courthouse first thing in the morning. Let's get some sleep."

"I'll take the cups," Jane said.

Rita reached for the tray. "Just put them on the tray. I'll take everything to the kitchen."

"I'd like the cups for a children's Sunday school snowflake project back home in Alabama. I save cups and toilet paper rolls wherever I go." Jane held up her shoulder bag large enough to hold the proverbial kitchen sink. "That's why I carry such a big purse." She grinned and deposited the cups in her purse.

Rita frowned and cocked her head. "I must enlist you on Christmas craft days. I have clean cups. You shouldn't have to use the dirty ones."

Rita reached out to take the cups, but Jane said, "No need to waste these. I'll rinse them out and save them."

"Looks like saving is the order of business and saving Mother from going to prison is number one," Cameo said. Even though she doesn't care about saving Topazus, we are now charged with saving her. A topic for tomorrow. I'm exhausted."

~

Jane sat silent a few moments to let the words of her morning devotion soak into her spirit. The scripture advised not storing treasures on earth where moth and rust destroy, and thieves break in and steal. Boy, did that ever apply to Topazus battling destructive mold, rats and a ring thief.

Even so, she confessed to seeing Topazus as a treasure.

Jane stepped to the window of her bed-and-breakfast room and admired the garden backdropped by the stately mansion. She sipped her spiced tea left over from breakfast. The cinnamon-orange flavor, a comforting balm.

Cameo's remark about having to save her mother who didn't care about saving Topazus puzzled Jane. Had she meant her words to be supportive or as an affront—an irritation—a bother? Where was Cameo's allegiance. Where was her treasure?

And did the paper Jane found tucked in the ledger

book that appeared to be a handwritten deed have value? She'd tried to show it to Robert last night, but Cameo and James arrived before she could. When she told him about the paper later last night, he'd said to wait and they'd look at it when things settled down. But things seemed to be stirring rather than settling.

After calling Adam regarding rats and mold, he had agreed to come with a specialist at eleven o'clock. At breakfast, Robert had asked Rita for a box he could use for shipping a gift. She produced a perfect box complete with bubble wrap. Jane helped Robert label and package the computer drive and the cups to send to his contact in Alabama for fingerprinting.

"Is this okay?" She had asked Robert. "I mean do we have to share what we find on this drive with the prosecutor?"

"If it's deemed a part of the investigation as to guilt or innocence of the accused, we do. But they likely have the same information and a lot more since they have Berdanier's computer and hard files. Getting a fingerprint off the drive may be of more value to us than what's recorded on it. Finding out who took it could reveal something about the web we're caught up in. Someone fears what's on that drive."

"What I don't get is why hide the drive? Why not just take it?"

"Maybe they didn't want to chance being in possession of it. Could have wanted to buy time in order to get first view and planned to retrieve it later. Could be other reasons."

"Whoever it is will be upset that it's gone," Jane said.

"And can't complain without showing their hand.

But from what we saw last night after downloading, the drive contains little more than a topic list. I doubt anyone is fretting over a cigar order receipt, or a pawnshop phone number in Myrtle Beach. I want you to read over the mineral rights information and ring theft report while I'm out."

Robert had gone with Cameo and James to first appearance and planned to mail the "gift box" on the way. Since there were no events at Topazus until the weekend, Rita had left after breakfast to tend to a catering job in Granite Ridge. The house was left unlocked in case Jane was able to contact an exterminator.

Settling in front of her laptop, Jane opened Berdanier's file downloaded to her computer. As Robert had said, there was not much content on the drive. She ran her cursor to the document she wanted to sink her teeth into: The Topazus Ring. The file contained a copy of two insurance claims, one for hurricane loss and one for the loss of the ring, both dated September 25, 2018. The claims read much the same but had different claim numbers:

The Topazus mansion incurred losses from a tree that fell against the house, causing damage to the outer wall and breaking a window. There was subsequent wind and water damage from rain to the floor and furnishings in the drawing room.

The glass display case housing the Topazus ring was cracked and broken and the ring missing as well as other small items of silver, the silver chests in the kitchen and dining room. Evidence of looting was documented.

The insurance estimate for the home repair and

content loss was $11,000. For the ring, $50,000.

"September, two thousand eighteen," Jane said aloud. She reached for her phone and pulled up the video she and Robert viewed the night before to double check the date.

The wedding couple was listed as Cindy and Greg Patterson. The video posted on May 19, 2019 which was well after the September 2018 date listed for the insurance claim on the ring. It was possible the video was taken earlier and posted long after the event. To confirm her suspicion that Rita still possessed the ring after it was reported stolen, she needed to know the couple's wedding date. She drummed her fingers against the desk, then slapped it.

"Wedding registries."

She searched popular sites couples used. Nothing until Amazon. Jane clapped and jumped from her seat.

"Cindy and Greg Patterson, wedding date: May 20, 2019, location Morgan City, South Carolina."

If they were the same couple and the ring in the video the real thing, insurance claims representatives might well be interested. Was Berdanier party to insurance fraud? Blackmail? Whistleblower? Did the disposition of the ring have something to do with the report Berdanier was ready to share?

But what if the wedding date listed was in error? She needed confirmation. Rita had a small office off the kitchen porch. There should be an appointment calendar.

With little thought, Jane set out on the garden path leading to the kitchen. The screen door slapped closed behind her. She scooted past brooms, mops and buckets with the strong smell of bleach and tripped on a pair of garden shoes as she entered Rita's tiny office.

Her desk was a small oak roll top with several cubby holes and drawers on one side. A current December calendar was on top of her desk. The second drawer rewarded her with a date book. She flipped to May. There it was, in big red letters, Patterson luncheon on May 19, 2019, the day before the wedding and eight months after the report of the stolen ring.

Was the ring stolen and then found? If the insurance money saved the estate from bankruptcy, how could the money be reimbursed? Estate representatives would be in a bind. Or was the ring never taken to begin with? Either way, keeping the ring was wrong and if Berdanier knew ... where was the ring now? It would be risky for Rita to keep it with her. But ...

She closed the drawer and checked the time. Her brother should arrive in thirty minutes. Rita had acted strange and rolled the ring in her gloves when Jane saw her in the dressing room after the tea party.

Jane hurried from the kitchen through the dining room into the main hall and mounted the stairs two at a time. Inside the lavender-scented dressing room, the curtains were drawn. The ceiling fixture presented only dim light. She drew back the room darkening curtains and daylight flooded in.

The room was furnished with a chest of drawers, a dresser with a mirror and jewelry box, a separate full-length mirror, and a clothing rack of men and women's period dress.

She lifted the lid on the jewelry box. A ring glittered. Her breath stalled, then released. Only the copy of the Topazus ring. She searched the dresser drawers. Fingered soft folds of undergarments. Pressed sachet packets that puffed floral scents. She carefully examined several pairs of gloves folded neatly in a bottom drawer. No hard object. She took pains to return everything as she'd found them.

The drawers in her mother's bedroom in Mobile were neat like these. Everything claimed a special place. Jane had put off going through her mother's things since she died. It seemed sacrilegious to tamper with her possessions and somehow, leaving them undisturbed made the loss of her presence less harsh. Not so final.

But this search for the ring could unlock crucial clues as to what lay behind Berdanier's murder. She stood, hands on hips, and scanned the room. "Ring. I feel it from the tips of my fingers to the ends of my toes, you are here somewhere."

She stepped to the closet; her shoes clicked against the floor, echoing across the room. The closet next to the fireplace was empty, dark and musty. She eyed the fireplace. Could there be a fake drawer in the mantle like the one in the library?

She ran her hand along the smooth, carved trim. "Robert rapped the mantle and the drawer popped open," she whispered. She gave the mantle a *smack*. Nothing. Maybe he hit a concealed release button? She ran her hands under the mantle and whacked it again.

"What are you doing?"

She whirled about, clutching her hands to her chest.

"Micah. You frightened me out of my wits. Uh …" She couldn't tell him she was convinced the Topazus ring was in the room. She tried to slow her pounding heart and prodded her brain to think of something plausible. The words spilled out. "My brother will be here shortly with a coworker to look into the mold and rat problem discovered in the drawing room. I thought I'd check for other rat or mold activity before they arrived."

He frowned. "I was in the garden and saw the curtains move." He stepped into the room.

The action made her uneasy. Gardening in the dead of winter? "I was checking for mold on the sills." *Change the subject.* "What kind of gardening do you do this time of year?"

"I turn the soil before spring planting. The winter cold kills unwanted weeds and rids it of pests."

Did he consider her a pest? Her pulse pounded in her ears. He walked to the windows opposite the fireplace. "If you're finished with your search for rats, I'll close the curtains. It helps to keep out the chill. The house is difficult to heat." He scowled, looked around the room then said, "I'll unlock the gate for your brother."

"I'd better go out front to meet him." Jane's breathing constricted. What was happening? She hurried from the room and down the stairs, leaving Micah behind her.

In that moment upstairs, Jane felt something sinister in the place. The words of Cameo's mother resounded in her ears. "The house is dark and evil."

Outside, she gulped in the fresh air as if she'd been smothered. The weather was chilly, yet her face prickled with perspiration. She leaned against a column by the front door, feeling foolish. What was wrong with her? Her imagination was taking over.

Lord, calm me down.

By the time her brother arrived in a van with *Restorers of the South* painted on the side, her pulse rate had returned to normal. Her brother introduced the tall, thin man with sandy blond hair with him as Butch Anderson.

She led the way inside. Micah was already in the dining room. His disturbing demeanor had changed. Or was it her perception? She introduced him. "Micah oversees the estate."

Micah acknowledged them and went directly to the spot Adam had found and touched the release button to open the concealed door.

"I worked in an old house where the owners turned a hidden space like this into an office," Butch said. He donned a headlamp, centered the light on his forehead and went inside.

"Adam, you said the mold was pervasive. You were right. This is bad." He shone his light all around. "And there are rats. No question." He stepped back out. "The mold can be cleaned with disinfectant and we can set traps for the rats, but that source of water has to be stopped first. I'd say, without looking at the entire roof, that at minimum the wood and flashing around the chimney needs replacing. And it may need a new roof. Honestly, any cleaning we do now would be temporary until the roof is repaired."

Micah pressed his lips into a straight line and shook his head. "We've been patching and making do for quite a while."

Butch clicked his tongue. "It may be to the point that repairs will cost more than rebuilding."

Had Berdanier intended to discuss that possibility with Cameo? Was he going to encourage selling to the developer?

"Can you write up the need and your recommendations?" Jane asked.

"I can. But it would be best to look around the other fireplaces while I'm here."

"There are two more spaces like this downstairs," Micah said. "One underneath the stairs backing the music room, and another in the drawing room that backs up to the library. Upstairs, the spaces beside the fireplaces are the closets." No wonder Rita uses a clothing rack instead of the closet.

Adam and Jane followed as Micah accessed a door that blended with the woodwork under the stairs and the door access in the drawing room blended with the wallpaper like the one in the dining room. Micah explained that the spaces had been used for storage but hadn't been used for some time.

Butch explored each space, reporting more mildew and rat signs and more sections of moisture and rot next to the chimneys. Upstairs had similar issues. After taking moisture readings, Butch went to his van to list his findings.

Jane and Adam spoke with Micah back in the main hall. "I'm going to cut fresh pine for the mantles. My wife wants me to bring some home too. Let me know if you need anything else." He handed both Adam and Jane his business card. She ran her finger over the letters printed on the card. Micah had been so helpful. Had she been foolish to fear him?

"Thank you for your help."

"It's my job to oversee the mansion." He shrugged and remained serious. "But the place needs more than I can give." He turned and exited out the back door.

Jane turned to Adam. "Thank you for coming and bringing Butch to conduct the inspection."

"He's good. He'll give a thorough, honest report."

"Cameo needs a straight up report." Her stomach tightened. Could she approach Adam? She had to try. "Can we be straight up?"

He pinched his brows together. "I suppose."

"We've been cordial, and it was fun seeing your boys and participating in activities yesterday. But I feel like we're tiptoeing around the enormous boulder sitting in the middle of the niceties and acting like it isn't there."

He fidgeted, bumping the fist of one hand against the palm of the other. "You want to revisit my not coming when mother was dying."

"Partly. But our estrangement goes further back. It was as if when Mom and Dad ceased being husband and wife, we ceased being brother and sister. I looked up to you as my big brother and ... you left me."

Adam folded his arms across his chest. "If you wanted me near you, why didn't you stay? Dad asked you to."

"But I couldn't leave mother. She would have been all alone."

"She moved in with Grandma and started a whole new career. Dad was the one left alone and I couldn't leave him."

"He remarried." Jane's response was blunt.

Adam straightened. "Two years after the divorce and they were only married six months before he died in the construction accident. So, I don't regret staying with him. You made your choice and I made mine."

"But to not see mother when she was so sick and

asking for you ..."

Adam began shaking his head before she could finish. "That's what I thought. You can't leave it alone."

The front door opened, and Butch said, "Here's the report. Can you call Micah back in?"

Jane snuffed back waterworks that burned her eyes and went to summon Micah. When she returned, Adam was gone.

Butch went over the report with both her and Micah. He gave an estimate on interior cleaning but highly recommended a roof inspection.

When finished, Jane walked Butch to the front door. Adam sat in the passenger seat of the van, leaning against the headrest. His eyes were closed, and so was the discussion of their relationship.

CHAPTER NINE

Jane lay like a limp rag on the bed in her room, staring at the ceiling. What an idiot. Adam wouldn't change, and she couldn't forget how he let down their mother and her.

She had watched, alone, as her mother died. Jane had kissed her mother's head one last time. Her sparse hair, like peach fuzz, brushed against her lips. Her once warm-toned complexion was gray. The cheeks sunken. Dark circles underscored her pleading, watery eyes. She no longer had the strength to use her voice to beg for Adam and ask where he was. Jane had lied. She said Adam had been delayed and was on his way. She begged her mother to hang on, hoping Adam would appear. But the beseeching eyes became a blank stare. The weak grip went slack. She was gone.

Adam's betrayal complete.

But why was she compelled to bring it up? Pulling her down and him with her. What was the point?

Was it Topazus? Katherine said the house made

her uneasy. Was that effect rubbing off on Jane? Pushing her into conflict? Jane had seen Micah as sinister. She was even convinced Rita still had the Topazus ring. Was she wrong?

A shiver took hold. She hugged her arms to her chest. If Topazus made Katherine feel this way, she could understand her not wanting to live in the house.

She examined the swirls on the ceiling, circles leading nowhere, starting and finishing in the same spot. She had set off on good footing with Adam and his boys but came full circle to the bitterness that put them at odds to begin with.

Rita had left salad and sandwich fixings in the refrigerator. The smell of her half-eaten tuna salad sandwich was no longer inviting and did not sit well on her stomach. She sat up, laid a napkin over the sandwich, and reached for the brochure about the brothers so at odds that they were willing to kill each other in the Civil War. They forgave each other. Had they been as close, before the war that divided them, as she had been with Adam?

He was her superhero when that horrid Paxton Sapp made fun of her protruding teeth, that braces later fixed. Adam had grabbed Paxton with fistfuls of his shirt and said, "You will envy her teeth when you don't have any." Paxton had steered clear of Jane after that and Adam escorted her home for weeks to make sure he did.

He was her defender. He'd promised to maintain contact after the divorce, but he had let her down. Christmas and summer visits lessened and then stopped. Baseball and sports camps took priority.

Conflicts end when people change. That's what the

brochure proclaimed. But conflicts started when Adam changed.

Lord, please change Adam back to the way he was.

There was a light rap at her door. "Jane?"

Robert was back, and she was lying down on the job. She bounded from the bed, tied her hair in a loose ponytail and opened the door. His expression was drawn.

"It's been a tiresome day." He crossed the room and sank into the upholstered side chair.

"Tell me about it." She pulled the desk chair out, angling it toward him.

"This is an unusual situation. James and Cameo are attorneys. However, both being so closely involved, know it is wise to use the criminal attorney recommended by James' law firm to represent Katherine. Bond was set at $75,000 but the lawyer argued it down to $25,000 citing Katherine as a no flight risk, with no criminal history, and substantial connections to the community."

"She's out now?"

"Yes. Until the preliminary hearing. The judge reviewed the complaint and determined the alleged facts indicate the defendant probably committed the murder."

"Just based on a police report? That doesn't seem fair."

"That's where court proceedings start. A murder occurred, and she seems the likely one who did it since it was her gun that killed Berdanier. Police are the fact gatherers. Now it's in the hands of the prosecutor who filed information that warranted the arrest." Robert blew out a puff of air. "Which means the defense has access to interviews and evidence collected thus far."

"Okay, so now what?"

"James and Cameo took Katherine to Crest Manor. Cameo wants to meet in the library, which is becoming our new workplace, around nine o'clock. I suspect James will be with her." He looked at her computer. "What did you find in the files on the thumb drive?"

"Uh ... I'm afraid I let you down." The hard chair back prodded her, and she shifted her position. That is what she had said her brother did to her—let her down.

"How's that?"

"I started looking over information from the drive about the ring and got waylaid." She looked down, avoiding eye contact. How could she be a PI intern if she didn't work on what she was assigned? She let her half-baked notion take over. Then her personal problems with her brother interfered.

"And?"

"I went searching for the ring."

"What happened that has you looking all guilt ridden?"

"I decided that Rita must have a record of the events she handles in her little office off the kitchen. I wanted to confirm the date of the bridesmaid's luncheon and compare it to the date on the insurance claim for the ring."

"Sounds like outstanding detective work to me. What did you find?"

Those words brought hope to her spirit.

"What I hoped for. An appointment calendar with the Patterson bridesmaid luncheon written on May nineteen. If the ring in the video was genuine, she was wearing it months after the claim."

Robert stood. "So, where is the ring now?"

"Remember when I went to change clothes after you told me about the search warrant Saturday?"

Robert nodded and twirled his hand in an out-with-it fashion.

"Bear with me," Jane said holding up a hand. "When I walked in the dressing room, Rita was standing at the window holding up her gloved hand with the ring catching the light. She was talking and didn't know I was there, muttering things about the ring and the garden. I felt weird listening and cleared my throat. When she heard me, she jerked her hands down." Jane stood to demonstrate. "She peeled off the gloves and then rolled them up and set them on the dresser."

"I assumed she was rolling the imitation ring up in the gloves. But now I wonder after seeing the video. Holding her hand up to the window, the ring lit up. Why jerk her hands down and conceal a fake ring?"

"A good observation." Robert paced. "She doesn't dare bring it out while Cameo or anyone of us would recognize it as the original."

"Cameo brought up insurance fraud at the luncheon and the ring was on Berdanier's list to discuss. They both apparently had suspicions."

Robert rubbed his chin. "If the theft report was false, they'd be in trouble with the insurance company."

"A good reason for the one who has the ring to fear being found out," Jane said. "So, I used rule number two and asked what if? What if Rita keeps the real ring in the dressing room? And what if there is a secret drawer in the fireplace like the one if the library?"

Robert frowned. "Can't you just say if you found

the ring or not?"

She emitted a long, heavy sigh. "No. I didn't find it. I'm trying to set the scene for what happened."

Robert slumped back in his chair. "Okay."

"I was poking and prodding around the fireplace in the dressing room, trying to see if there was a hidden drawer, when I heard this menacing voice say, 'What are you doing?' Scared me silly. I whirled around and it was Micah."

"I'm guessing you were relieved."

"No." Her voice strained. "The way he looked at me, gave me the creeps. His eyes seemed to go dark and sinister."

"Guilt that he caught you?"

"Maybe, but he didn't come across as his general nice self. I don't know if it was him, me, or the house. I feel different in the house." It was Jane's turn to pace. "It's hard to explain, but that place changes people."

She pivoted on her heel and picked up the brochure. "It says right here," she flicked the pamphlet, "Conflicts end when people change. Whoever wrote this, got it backwards. People change and conflict escalates."

"I had opened the curtains for more light and Micah didn't approve. He stepped into the room to close the curtains and I felt as if the walls were closing in. I said my brother was on his way with an exterminator and I was checking for more rat signs. He must have thought me weird, but I left that room at a near run. When I got outside, it felt like I'd just broken the surface after holding my breath underwater. My lungs screamed for air."

"Sounds like a panic attack."

"Precisely. But why? It was strange. Micah was helpful and couldn't have been nicer after my brother arrived to check the house. He knows where secret passages are and how to access them."

Robert leaned forward and rested his chin on his hands. "Then he must know about the hidden drawer in the library. What places did he show you today?"

"Besides the hidden space in the dining room there is one under the stairs that backs up to the music room and one on the drawing room fireplace wall that backs up to the library. Micah said the spaces were designed for extra storage. The inspector found rodent issues, serious mold and water leak problems around the chimneys and left a detailed report."

"Huh. Pervasive mold and leaks. Yet Rita hires a guy who says everything is fine." Robert steepled his fingers and went silent.

Jane went silent too. Behind the fancy facade of wallpaper, lovely furnishings and sweet-smelling potpourri, there was a malignancy growing in the house that was being ignored. Why cover it up?

"Why pretend nothing is wrong?" Robert blurted.

Jane went goose bumpy. "I was wondering the same thing."

"Whatever the reasoning, Berdanier had a plan to discuss the mold—among other things. Was this the problem someone wanted to be certain Berdanier didn't expose?"

~

Robert paced a trail to the window and back again. They had acquired information, asked questions, and come up with hypotheses. He folded his arms and pressed his back against the door frame. They needed direction, wisdom—truth. "We need to pray."

Jane laced her fingers together and held them up. "In my morning devotion, I read about a blind Paralympic runner. A veteran sprinter tethered his fingers to the blind runner's and used verbal cues to guide him. Robert, it's a picture of guidance available to us if we stop and ask."

Closing his eyes, Robert envisioned himself as the blind athlete being guided by faith in the hands of the veteran. "I needed that reminder." He inhaled then released his breath slowly, clearing and calming his mind.

"And Lord we do seek your guidance in this case. Please order our steps to find the truth behind the death of Alfred Berdanier."

They both remained silent.

Topazus characters, their concerns and issues fanned out like playing cards, then gradually settled where Robert could focus on each.

He waited. Expectant. Two words took shape.

Motive.

Opportunity.

"Jane get ready to write."

She collected her pen and pad and settled at her desk. They had discovered a working rhythm. Instinctively she knew to let him think out loud, listen, and then summarize the ideas.

"A man has been murdered. The police have a suspect, Katherine. Indications are strong that she committed the crime, but my gut says she didn't."

"We're in the same scenario as our last case," Jane said.

She was right. The gun used to kill the victim in

the murder case they investigated last month belonged to their client. Circumstantial evidence. "And in both cases the defendant claims their innocence," Robert said.

"Therefore …"

"Therefore, we look at motive and opportunity. I believe we had lunch in the murderer's presence on Friday." Tossing ideas to Jane was like bouncing a basketball off a backboard. The ideas hit and then sprang from a different direction, giving a new perspective.

"Katherine." Jane wrote her name down. "Why her?"

Robert shoved his hands in his pockets and plodded along his carpet trail. "The forensics report we received in information from the prosecutor places the distance and angle of the shot to be from the wooded trail near the gate. Katherine could easily have accessed that path using the electric cart. Ballistics showed the bullet that shot Berdanier was from Katherine's gun."

Jane tapped the end of the pen to her lips. "She is reportedly a crack shot. Cameo saw her coming up the river walk but she may have been returning the gun by the back door."

"There's the opportunity, but what about motive?"

"Katherine threatened Berdanier," Jane said.

"Berdanier said, 'Don't shoot the messenger,' and she said he shouldn't bank on that. Perhaps Berdanier had unwittingly opened the door to his own demise. Katherine knew she was competent enough to be successful."

"What she said could be considered a threat. But … she didn't say she would kill him."

"Write that she made a caustic statement."

Jane wrote then said, "Katherine supported the sale to Chandler Development. Did she need Berdanier out of the way to get what she wanted?"

"She said she had no vote in the matter," Robert said.

"But was that a statement of disdain or fact? She might not have legal ownership but certainly let everyone know how she felt."

Jane was right. Katherine did not hesitate to make her feelings known. "In her estimation," Robert said, "investing in the house was throwing good money after bad."

"And she believed the house was evil and gave her headaches," Jane said. "After the vibes I had in the house today, she might have something."

Robert stopped pacing. "Maybe the house *is* evil in the sense it can harm you physically due to the mold and mildew. It threatens mental wellbeing with toxic exposure." He peered out the window at a spindly, leafless crepe myrtle tree. "Retribution. Add that to motive. By ending control of the trust, she'd have the satisfaction of ending her father-in-law's plan to keep Topazus from her through legal channels."

Jane's eyes lit up. She waggled her pen at Robert. "Berdanier irritated Katherine by dragging his feet about the mold inspection. By allowing the cover up, there'd be no reason to consider the developer's offer to repair and rebuild Topazus."

"Then she's sent over the edge when Berdanier brings up historical preservation and heirs' property. Either could cause acquisition red tape and make Chandler Development back out."

"But," Jane frowned, "if she kills Berdanier, that puts Cameo in control. And Cameo seems to be on the side of preservation."

"Maybe Katherine felt she could reason with her daughter. But it does weaken her as a suspect," Robert said.

"And Berdanier seemed to be open to listening to the Chandler proposal since Dean was invited to the luncheon." Jane scribbled more notes.

A redbird lit in the barren tree and cocked his head. Robert's stomach rumbled. "Look at the birds of the air."

"What?" Jane turned toward the window.

"Birds. The Bible says to look at the birds who don't reap or sow. They take a day at a time and don't worry about tomorrow." He scrubbed his hand over his stubble beard and his stomach grumbled. "But man, with his issues of greed, lust, jealousy revenge—you name it—has made it hard to appreciate today. Like us cooped up in this room, working."

"We have a murder on our hands."

"Yup, but I'm hungry. We can talk over food. I know a place to eat—actually, the only place. Grab your jacket we're going to town."

~

"Morgan City," Robert said, as they passed the city limit sign about eight miles from the Topazus plantation. "Cameo explained that this was once the county seat of now defunct Clark County. Currently, the town is dubbed a community in Bennett County."

"Too bad Clark County was dissolved but at least the Morgan name remains," Jane said.

"When places bear a person's name, I always think

of my grandfather, who lectured me about the value of a good name."

"A good name, rather than things, lasts from generation to generation," Jane said

"The name may last but not necessarily the good part." Robert countered and went reticent. The Grey name handed to Robert was a good name. A name that stood for honesty and trust in Pine Bluff, Alabama. It was debatable whether he'd kept it that way. The stain on his record as a lawman, though cleared, he could not erase. Negative impressions seem to stick more than the positive. Human nature.

"It seems the Morgan name is still good around here." Jane nodded toward the factory on the next block with Morgan Cotton Gin in huge letters.

"I imagine Morgan City qualifies as a one-horse town with the cotton gin their only industry."

"I used to think the saying meant the town was so small it only had one horse," Jane said.

Robert tilted his head in her direction. "You know what it *does* mean?"

"It refers to a town so small that the people only need wagons and carriages that require one horse."

"You're a bundle of information. It's nice having you around to keep me versed in trivia."

"Thanks, I think. I read everything I could find on the history of Topazus after Cameo invited us. Morgan City is a two-industry town when you include Topazus as a tourist attraction and working cotton farm."

"No question the town is influenced by cotton. Case in point," he said pulling up to the Cotton Boll Café and parking in front. "At three o'clock in the afternoon, if there was such a thing as a noon rush, then we avoided it.

Inside, the decor promised to be one that would interest Jane with its walls of exposed old brick and framed photos of the town during more affluent times. Robert perused them with her. One picture showed the town with shops open, sidewalks bustling with customers, and cars from the 1950s lined the street.

"Look. Here's one of Topazus with azaleas in bloom and girls dressed in gowns and bonnets."

"Hi folks," a young woman greeted them wearing a purple shirt with Cotton Boll Café printed in bright pink letters. "My name is Madison. Sit where you like, you have the place to yourself."

"Thank you. You have some interesting old photos here."

"They show much of the town's history."

Robert chose a table near the photos Jane was examining. "We are staying at the Topazus Bed-and-Breakfast," Robert said.

"I love that place. I was a Topazus Belle when I was in high school." She placed menus on the table. "Hard to believe Mr. Berdanier was murdered out there."

"Did you know Mr. Berdanier?"

She nodded. "I worked here last summer and met him then. He always kept to himself, reading his paper. But he started talking to me more after he found out I was a geology major at USC."

"What line of work are you interested in with that degree?" Jane asked.

"I'll work with my dad. He has a granite mining company. Mr. Berdanier was negotiating a mineral lease with him," she shrugged, "but I guess that won't happen now."

Robert shot a quick glance toward Jane.

"The river trout here is excellent, but we're all out."

"Uh ... well, that's disappointing. Now you have me wanting fish. What else do you have?" Robert asked.

"We're known for our low country boil. There's seafood in it and a whole bunch of other stuff. Our totally yummy homemade sourdough bread comes with it."

Robert looked at Jane, "Totally yummy okay with you?"

"Absolutely. Madison, you sold me," Jane said, and handed her menu to the waitress. "The mineral lease, was it going to be on the Topazus property?"

"Yes ma'am. Mr. Berdanier was the trustee for the estate. Geologic information indicates a unique granite outcropping on the site. The estate owner ought to look into it. I'll put your order in. What drinks can I bring you?"

They ordered waters and were left to contemplate this latest revelation.

"You asked me to research mineral rights. I haven't even read Berdanier's file yet. Sorry I got off track."

"If Berdanier was thinking of leasing mineral rights, I wonder if there was a side-bar deal that Cameo suspected?" Robert drummed his fingers on the table. "Cameo mentioned getting a call about mineral leasing when she attacked Berdanier's management skills. Let's examine her motive and opportunity."

"It's weird to consider Cameo as a suspect," Jane said pulling her pen and pad from her purse.

"Suspects come in all shapes, sizes, genders and some are weird."

"Thus, everyone's a suspect until they're not a suspect. I've got it written right here." She thumped her pen on the pad.

Robert propped his elbows on the table. "Cameo is heir of the property that has been in her family for seven generations. But the estate was held in trust with a successor trustee, Berdanier, who she believed was mismanaging the estate. When I retrieved her briefcase from her car last night, I saw a highlighted article about trustees and mismanagement on the backseat. So, she had concerns."

"She also alluded to insurance fraud, and his letting finances get out of hand," Jane said. "With him out of the way she could take over before he ran the estate into the ground."

"Hmm. And with this information about a mineral lease, did she suspect him of lining his own pockets?"

Jane lit up like she was about to tell him he'd won the lottery. "Cameo said she was contacted regarding mineral leasing and didn't like being kept in the dark." Jane spoke softly as Madison brought their drinks. "It could involve her father."

"Your order will be out in a jiffy," she said, placing drinks on the table.

"Madison, you said your father runs a granite mining company. What's his name and the name of the company?"

"Roger Underwood. His company is Underwood Granite."

"As in kitchen counters?" Jane asked.

"He mines a lot of aggregate for road and highway

construction, but he does quarry granite slabs."

"You think the Topazus property had granite suitable for mining?"

"Possibly. A core sampling would have to be done and environmental regulations met."

"The whole process sounds interesting."

"It is. Rocks of all kinds, that's my thing."

"It's wonderful you've found your niche."

"Thanks. I'll have your dinner right out."

Madison sashayed back to the kitchen.

Jane cocked a brow at Robert.

"Roger Underwood," Robert said. "That's the name Cameo dropped that got a rise out of Berdanier."

"And the needling went both ways."

"Cameo is smart. She can dish it out, but she's also known as a hot-head when her buttons are pushed."

"Enough to kill?" Jane asked.

"Think of her opportunity. She takes an electric cart, goes to Crest Manor to check on her mother while we wait for her in the library. She claims her mother is returning from the river walk after she looks for her. But did she take the gun, shoot Berdanier, and return it before her mother returned? She could have."

Jane's eyes widened, and her voice came out in a breathless whisper. "Then joined us back in the library. She seemed upset."

"Which could be attributed to the upsetting luncheon conversation. Remember, this is conjecture."

She pressed her hand to her heart. "Okay. I'll remember. Conjecture. You painted a believable picture though."

"Here you go, folks." Madison arrived with a tray of two steaming food platters and a breadbasket.

"Crushed red pepper on the table."

"This smells wonderful. What's in it?" Robert asked.

"Low country boil has sausage, shrimp, crab, potatoes and corn," she recited. "A whole meal in one."

They dug in and enjoyed their meal for a moment when Jane chuckled.

"What's so funny?"

"If James were here, he'd be telling us how to make low country boil."

"And he could expound on the proper way to season it," Robert said, pushing the red pepper her way.

"Are we being unkind talking about him?"

"Nope." He bit into his corn and dabbed at the butter on his chin. "Character analysis is constructive. For instance, your telling Madison she'd found her niche, sparked envy in you. Here was a gal who was not only majoring in a profession she loved but also set with a job in her field."

Jane looked down. "Scary. You knew what I was thinking again."

"Don't worry. I'm not clairvoyant. I just relate to career direction veering off course."

"However," Jane looked him in the eye, "here we sit."

Jane had shared how a boyfriend who later dropped her had convinced her to switch her major to elementary ed. "You were cut out for history and research and wound up teaching little kids."

"And you left behind a career in law enforcement and wound up a PI."

"Go figure." He offered a small smile. "Where were we?"

Jane brightened. "James Know-It-All Parsons. Analyze him as a suspect. I shall write and eat at the same time."

"James Parsons, a lawyer, who shares knowledge willingly on many subjects besides law. The son of Rita and Dean Parsons who have separate agendas regarding Topazus and James sides with his mother."

"And he helps with his mother's catering business. I might term him a renaissance man."

"What is that anyhow?" Robert asked.

"I think of it as a person who appreciates a variety of things and has skills and knowledge in many fields."

"I'd define him as cocky and irritating." Robert tore off a piece of bread. "Note that I am only buttering a piece of bread, not the whole thing."

"You're a good learner and Madison is right. The bread is yummy."

Robert pointed to Jane's notes. "Under opportunity, put down that he discovered the body."

"But why kill Berdanier?"

"He seems attached to Cameo. Maybe kill Berdanier, marry Cameo who now controls the estate and he becomes master? Maybe he sees something lucrative in owning the estate that we are not aware of." Robert said.

"He knew where Katherine kept the squirrel gun."

"Everyone at the luncheon heard that," Robert said.

"True. But think of opportunity for James. He disappeared after the luncheon. Said he was on the phone with a business call. But he could have taken a cart to Crest Manor while Katherine was on her walk."

"So, he takes the gun, kills Berdanier, and returns it. Then gets in his car and pretends to be upset at finding the body?"

Jane tilted her head. "He does know all."

Madison checked on them and refreshed their waters.

"Shall we analyze Rita?" Jane brandished her pen in one hand and her fork in the other.

"Rita, the substitutionary mistress. She is the former girlfriend of Cameo's father, but Morgan married Katherine and Rita married Dean."

"However," Jane said, "after James came along Rita and Dean divorced and now Dean dates Katherine and is representing the developers who want to purchase the estate. The perfect plot line for a television soap opera."

"Don't forget Rita's catering business is attached to Topazus. She has a vested interest in the place and must feel she deserves credit for keeping the estate afloat."

"Is she so attached that she would get rid of someone who threatened her position?"

"Maybe she interpreted Berdanier's giving audience to developers as a threat to her job."

"That video concerns me. And the strange way she acted when I walked in the dressing room. Why hide the ring if it was just the copy?"

"And if she has the original ring," Robert said, "did she take it for insurance and Berdanier found out? She could be looking at felony charges."

"So, she kills Berdanier because he was a threat to her livelihood and could get her in legal trouble. What about opportunity?"

"She went into the kitchen after the luncheon. She could have gone to Crest Manor on a cart, grabbed the gun, shot him, put the gun back, and returned to the mansion."

"She claimed to be in the dining room when James came in with the news," Jane said, writing on her pad.

Working with Jane had his mental juices flowing. "Let's consider Dean Parsons. He is liaison for Chandler Development who wants to purchase the Topazus estate. He seems to have only one person in his corner, Katherine. The company checks out as legit and is generous with their offer to relocate the mansion and preserve what they can of the main house, the church and tree. In exchange, he'd likely earn a sizeable commission."

Jane took a bite of food and munched as she wrote. "Okay. What's Dean's reason to get rid of Berdanier?"

"It might parallel Katherine's reason. If Berdanier was dabbling into mineral rights and heir's property, it could kill the deal."

"He might have financial need making it necessary to remove Berdanier from the dealings."

"And financial need could be the same for Katherine. She buddies up with Dean and they both benefit from the sale." Jane said. "What about opportunity for Dean?"

"He said he was on his way to Columbia for a meeting when he received a call from Katherine about the murder. But maybe he never left. He kills Berdanier and waits nearby to make it appear he's been gone."

Robert helped himself to more bread and offered some to Jane. "This little restaurant is a delicious find."

"Delicious food makes me think of Rita's sidekick, Mary Sue Sutton." Jane said.

"I learned from Horace Baxter that she used to work for Leo Calhoun who became state senator and

Berdanier was a frequent visitor. She left under apparent awkward circumstances. There was friction between her and Berdanier, evidenced by his dig about stealing masters. Was he holding potential scandal over her head?"

"Get rid of him out of revenge?" Jane speculated.

"She could have stolen away from the kitchen on a cart having learned about Katherine's rifle. Shot him and returned. I wonder if she is also an expert shot?" Robert leaned back in his chair. "Who's left of our prime suspects?"

"Micah."

Robert ordered coffees and looked over Jane's notes. She had done a nice job of putting their theories into concise statements. He pushed the notes back to her. "I wish you had been around the many times I've struggled over writing investigative reports and summaries."

Jane rewarded him with a smile that lit up her brown eyes. Brown eyes with flecks of green. Huh. He hadn't noticed before.

She held up her pen. "I'm waiting."

"Uh … yes. Micah. His family has been on the estate for seven generations. He is educated and has invested himself in this property. Even though he has no proof of ownership, he has been faithful to oversee the farm and household."

"And if the paper I saw was a legal deed—"

"Micah may have legal claim to part of the estate. What if he believed Berdanier knew it and was holding out on him?"

Jane stirred cream into her coffee and set her spoon on the saucer with a clank. "The thought of a developer coming in and pushing him from his home and livelihood may have punched his buttons."

"Same fear if he suspected Berdanier was turning to mineral exploration rather than cotton."

"Humiliation can stir powerful emotion," Jane said. "Berdanier criticized his ability in front of everyone."

Robert leaned forward and grasped his cup, feeling its warmth. "An important point. As far as opportunity, Micah said he was replacing fluorescent light bulbs at the pavilion after lunch. But when I noticed some lights still didn't work on Sunday, Micah said those lights needed ballasts. His alibi could be true, but if he's lying, he could have gone to Crest Manor and accessed the gun during that time."

"Cameo seems to appreciate Micah. Could he have wanted Berdanier out of the way so she would take over and secure his position at Topazus?"

"Possibly. I had the feeling Micah wanted to tell me something the night of the bonfire."

"He gave me the willies in the dressing room," Jane said.

"Whatever our suspicions, we need to keep them to ourselves for now."

Robert had prayed for guidance and direction. Brainstorming with Jane had helped establish plausible motives and opportunities among suspects.

But now Lord, where to next?

CHAPTER TEN

Jane grabbed Robert's arm. "Did you hear that?"

"Probably rats."

"Exactly." She was certain she heard a bumping noise when they entered the library. The dim wall sconce lighting from the hall cast sinister shadows across the room. She shivered. "This place increasingly gives me the creeps."

She hated to be a wimp, but on the garden path with Robert earlier, Micah had startled her when he materialized out of the dark.

"Micah. Hello." Robert had said. "I didn't see you there."

"Cameo called and asked that I open the house for you. I'm dealing with some non-functioning Christmas lights out front."

"I just heard from her too. Thank you for stopping what you were doing to let us in."

Micah opened the door and then had disappeared

back into the shadows.

"Let's turn on the floor lamps." Robert's footsteps fell soft on the oriental rug and Jane was close on his heels.

"Cameo said she was getting her mother settled at Crest Manor. James had business to tend to but would meet us at nine. We're to help ourselves to sandwich fixings that Rita left in the fridge."

"After our late lunch," Jane said, "I'm not hungry but Rita is a hostess who thinks of everything."

"Hmm."

"You don't think so?"

Robert tapped his index finger to his lips and flicked on the floor lamps in the corners of the room. He pulled out a business card, wrote on it and handed it to her.

He had written: *Could be human rats we heard. Speak in generalities.*

"Our objective is to take in more information than we give out," Robert said softly.

"Should I add that to my list of rules?" Jane whispered.

"Yes, and put a star by it."

Did he think she needed a star to remember to listen? Did he think she talked too much?

"Lights definitely help," Robert said in a normal voice. He whispered, "Show me the document that looked like a deed."

Jane located the ledger book and flipped to the loose document tucked in the book. She only had a glimpse before but now saw that the paper was signed by Morgan Danford Clark, Sr, October 9, 1858. She handed the paper to Robert. "So many books. I wonder if the owners ever had a chance to read them all?" Jane said.

"That would be quite an undertaking," Robert said, while examining the document. He held up the paper and mouthed, "It looks genuine." He tucked the paper inside his jacket and handed her the book to return to the shelf. "Did you say you lost an earring?" Robert pointed upstairs and to his ring finger.

"I did. I could have lost it upstairs in the dressing room."

"I'll help you look."

Upstairs they continued to keep their voices low. Jane went to the fireplace. "When I looked for the ring, I checked for any hidden switches and even slapped the mantle like you did downstairs. And that's when Micah caught me snooping."

Robert began running his hand over the mantle. "Did you examine those dishes of smell-good stuff?"

"Potpourri. No, I didn't." She plunged her fingers into the dish on the mantle with a surge of anticipation. Nothing. She checked the one on the dresser. Nothing hard. Only the crispy edges of dried flowers. "Rats. Not here," she said in a hoarse whisper.

"We know where the rats are." Robert maintained a deadpan expression and continued his search around the fireplace.

She wrinkled her nose. "Funny."

Jane lifted the lid of the jewelry box she'd looked in earlier that day and took out the replica of the topaz ring. Slipping it on her finger, she held it up to the overhead light.

Robert peered over her shoulder. "It looks impressive to me."

"But compared to the ring I saw her wearing after the tea, I am persuaded that Rita has the original."

"And she wouldn't dare keep it on her," Robert said. "I agree that it's likely hidden up here," he shook his head, "but no luck on finding any secret releases around the fireplace."

The back door rattled, and Cameo's voice called out, "Hello? Robert, you here?"

"Up here." He called out. To Jane he said, "Time to hear the latest."

Jane returned the ring to the box, and they hurried downstairs.

"Jane is missing an earring and thought she may have lost it upstairs."

"No luck." Jane splayed out her hands.

"Hopefully it turns up, Jane."

The rear door opened, and James walked in. "Hello all. Hope I'm not late."

"No. I just got here myself." Cameo said.

"And Jane and I haven't been waiting long either."

Cameo shrugged out of her jacket. James helped. "I'm famished."

James handed Cameo her jacket and said, "You go ahead. I know where mother put the food for us. I'll bring it to the library."

"Thank you." Cameo's voice carried an extra appreciative edge. Friends to lovers? Having him stick by her side during such a troublesome time would make a friendship more endearing.

"How is your mother?" Jane asked.

"Depressed."

"Should you leave her alone?" Robert asked.

"She said she just wanted to get a shower and sleep

in her own bed tonight."

"Sleeping in her own bed should be a relief after what she has been through," Jane said.

"Absolutely. Berdanier may have upset her, but it's ludicrous to think she'd murder him. I don't believe she did it."

As difficult as the arrest must have been, Cameo standing by her mother could be a positive side effect to take the edge off bitter feelings. Would something drastic have to happen to mend her relationship with her brother?

"What do you think of her attorney?" Robert asked Cameo but got his answer from James, carrying in a tray of sandwiches and drinks.

"First rate. He has fifteen years of experience in criminal courts and a superb relationship with the judges. Cameo can tell you, that's a plus."

The guy even had the words for others to speak.

Cameo obliged. "A definite plus. And your mother is a blessing. She continues to amaze with her thoughtfulness. Please thank her for us."

"Will do. But you'll probably be able to thank her yourself before I see her. She is catering a Christmas party in Granite Ridge and has a wedding reception. But she'll be back at Topazus by Friday, if not before, to make sure breakfast is satisfactory."

"Robert, Cameo and I are the only ones staying here right now," Jane said. "We can fend for ourselves for breakfast."

"True. There is no need for Rita to worry with us when she is thirty miles away," Cameo said.

James shook his head and placed the tray on the library table. "The distance is nothing to her. Hosting at

Topazus is her thing. Trust me, she will want to be sure you are fed properly. She has Mary Sue scheduled to handle your breakfast until she's able to be here."

Everyone took food to their chairs.

"I want to know about the mold and mildew report from your brother," Cameo said.

"Adam came with a coworker who specializes in dealing with mold clean up and pest control. He prepared a report." Jane reached in her purse and handed the paper to Cameo. "He found extensive mold and leaks around the chimneys that is affecting both the upstairs and downstairs along with rodent infestation."

Cameo frowned as she read over the report. "Rats? This should have been taken care of some time ago. The report cites long-standing pervasive damage. How did this get past Berdanier?"

"The leaks could be recent ones." James held up his bottled water as if it presenting an object lesson. Jane prepared to be enlightened. "Without water, molds die, but the spores can regenerate, growing new colonies of mold." He didn't disappoint.

"Strange that Rita received a report stating the house was clear of mold," Robert made certain Rita's mold inspection was not forgotten.

"I guess we know who not to use next time," James said and snickered.

Cameo scowled at James. She was in no joking mood. She shifted to her no-nonsense lawyer mode. James turned his attention to his sandwich.

"Thank you for setting up this inspection, Jane," Cameo said.

"Micah was helpful. He pointed out the concealed spaces next to the fireplaces."

"I see that from the report. I vaguely remember seeing a storage space where Dad kept extra chairs in the drawing room but didn't know about the others." She looked at James, who shrugged as though clueless. Cameo raised a brow. "I need to be shown those spaces myself."

"Access is cleverly hidden and hard to see," Jane said. "Robert can I use the flashlight on your phone?" He pulled up the app and Jane led the way down the hall, shining the light under the stairs. Pressing next to the trim as Micah did, a panel slid open and they peered inside.

"It is musty, and I can see the mold," Cameo said.

Jane showed her the other places. Cameo inspected and turned to James.

"Micah knew about these hidden areas, and your mother was unaware?" Cameo face was pinched, her tone carried a sour edge.

James raised his shoulders. "First I've seen them. It must be why Brandon's inspection missed the mold since he wasn't able to access everything."

They walked back to the library and Cameo dropped into one of the upholstered chairs and huffed out a puff of air. "Robert, I wanted you and Jane to have an amazing holiday but since the estate is now mine to manage, there is more work I need you to do."

"The law enforcement people finished with Berdanier's office. Robert, I want you to research anything regarding mineral rights and leasing in Berdanier's records. Jane, you like history. Topazus is on the historical register. Look into historical preservation rules and regulations—anything pertinent to Topazus."

Jane nodded, clamping her hands together, but her stomach went queasy. Preservation was a topic she'd gladly research for Cameo, but what if she overlooked important information? She didn't care to invoke her disfavor.

"Are we going to be able to get into his office?" Robert asked.

"You can use my key. Berdanier was divorced but his son, Ed, who lives in Chicago is beneficiary. I spoke to him on the phone. He said that per his father's instructions, he was to have his father cremated and the cremains scattered in the parking lot behind his office so he would always be underfoot."

"Sounds like him. Devising a way to irritate people even after he's gone," James said.

"Berdanier was annoying. I didn't care for his techniques, but he was no fool. I have his computer and started reading through his topics of concern, so the drive that went missing is no big deal, but this is." She picked up the report Jane had given her and whacked it against the chair arm. "I see now why mold was on his list. This problem and others must be addressed to see if Topazus can be saved."

James leaned back in the chair, propped one leg over the opposing knee and jiggled his foot. "Of course, Topazus can be saved. All you need is bleach."

Cameo brows drew together. "Bleach won't fix leaks."

James deflated.

Cameo turned back to Robert. "Regarding Berdanier's law office, Ed said to take what I needed. He plans to box and store the rest in order to close out the office lease by the end of the year. You and Jane go through his files before they're sealed." Cameo offered a softened expression toward James. "I'm certain Pruitt is well-versed in handling mother's defense, but I want us to be available to him and not be tied up searching Berdanier's records."

Bam. The rear door slammed against the wall.

Heavy footsteps pounded down the hallway.

Dean Parsons appeared in the door of the library. Face flushed. Eyes wide. His hands fisted at his sides, he growled, "Katherine was arrested and put in jail. Why am I just finding out?"

James let his foot drop to the floor, and he sat erect. "You were at an out-of-town meeting. It just happened last night. She's out on bail."

Dean's white hair deepened the dark glare focused on James.

"How can anyone believe she murdered Berdanier? This never would have happened if you," he jabbed his index finger at James, "and your mother didn't have a stranglehold on this place. But you can put away your devious plans. I'm turning myself in. I killed him."

~

Jane sat frozen, only moving enough to observe the reaction of others in the room.

Robert choked on his lemonade, James' mouth gaped open, and Cameo's face twisted into a frown.

Dean's retreating footsteps echoed down the hall. When the back door opened and banged shut, James jumped up, as if slapped. "I have to call Pruitt."

Cameo reached out and touched James' arm, her eyes filled with concern. "You don't seriously think ..."

James raked both hands through his hair. "Your mother didn't confess. I don't know what to think." He twisted his head around to look at Cameo. "Dad said he went to his real estate office after the luncheon. But did he? He was with Katherine in the cart she keeps at Crest Manor when Agent Kelley was questioning people."

Cameo slumped in her chair. "I wondered how he got back so fast."

James wrung his hands and walked toward the Christmas tree, muttering. "He's always been jealous of Topazus." He turned and said, "Making money from the sale of the estate thrilled my father. Berdanier digging up issues that would make Chandler Development back out could have put him over the edge."

Jane squirmed in her seat. Bizarre. They seemed to be presenting a case worthy of a prosecutor, incriminating Dean. James laid out a convincing argument. Shouldn't he be stating reasons he believed his father was innocent?

"Emotions take over and people are capable of shocking acts they wish they could take back," Cameo said.

"Which includes confessions." Robert's statement presented an alternate explanation for Dean's actions. Not hearing it from James or Cameo surprised Jane.

James flexed his fingers repeatedly, stared in Robert's direction, and then hurried out of the room.

Cameo grabbed her purse. "I'd better go with him."

"Go ahead," Robert said. "Jane and I will take care of things here."

"Thank you. Keep track of your time. Jane, check with your brother about sending a reputable roofer for an estimate."

She hurried to the door, stopped and turned back around. "And have the man who wrote the report set traps. I want the rats out."

Jane shuddered from the effects of the grenade that had exploded in the room, spewing emotional shrapnel.

Robert sucked in air and let it blow out in a slow, steady stream. "I'm convinced we're dealing with more rats than the four-legged variety."

CHAPTER ELEVEN

The morning sky had changed from clear blue to an overcast gray by the time Robert met Jane in the garden before breakfast. She stood by a camellia bush full of bright pink blossoms, her back to him.

"Morning."

Jane turned around and responded with her own cheerful, "Morning."

She looked different. Her hair. It was straight. Broom straw straight. "What happened to your hair?"

"I straightened it."

"No kidding. Did you lay your head on an ironing board?"

"No silly. I used an iron, but not that kind. A hair straightening iron. My hair will actually stay straight for a while in cold weather. So, I'm taking advantage. Like it?"

Now there was a loaded question. "I say whatever you like just tickles me to death." He'd move from hair to something easier—murder investigation.

"I talked to Cameo this morning. She said that after Dean confessed, he was questioned and held overnight at the Bennett County Sheriff's Office. His original story will be checked against his confession to see if facts line up."

Jane shook her head. "He either lied to begin with, or he's lying now. Will Cameo be at breakfast?"

"No." Robert motioned toward a wrought-iron bench in a small alcove off the garden path. "She went to Granite Ridge with her mother." He picked up a stick, brushed leaves from the seat and they both sat down. "Katherine was upset Dean confessed and believes he is trying to protect her."

"That was my first thought. But the way James talked and Cameo too, they seemed to believe it was plausible that Dean committed the murder."

"Or wishful thinking on James' part. Father and son radiated contention at the luncheon the other day."

"Well, Dean must really care for Katherine to confess, guilty or not."

"False confessions, if his is false, happen for various reasons, but my bet is he cares for Katherine enough to take her place. And he can be assured he won't see his son make the same sacrifice for him."

"Could his confession help cast reasonable doubt that Katherine shot Berdanier?"

"Possibly, but it could backfire and show he fears she's guilty," Robert said.

"Berdanier's death has brought out all kinds of emotions."

"And that's why murder is referred to as a crime of passion." He grasped the stick, rough and biting in his hand, and tossed it. "Humans are complicated. Come on. Let's fuel up. We have a busy morning ahead, poring over Berdanier's files."

Mary Sue was placing coffee cups next to place settings for two in the dining room.

"The coffee smells great, Mary Sue," Jane said.

"Any chance we can eat in the kitchen?" Robert asked. "It's overkill to be seated at such a long table with only two people."

"Rita might frown on it ... but," she lifted the coffee cups back off the table and grinned, "if you'd really like to."

"Lead the way."

They followed Mary Sue through the two-way kitchen door.

"Have a seat." She set the cups on a small kitchen table with four chairs where a half-full cup of coffee and a book rested. "I'll enjoy the company."

Jane looked at the book title. "Anna Karenina. A classic."

"Have you read it?" Mary Sue asked and retrieved the coffeepot. "It's required reading for the on-line college class I'm taking."

"It was required reading for me too in freshman English. Are you in a degree program?"

"I'm taking the basics right now, but I hope to enter nursing." She filled their cups. "It's slow going. I have to work and take one class at a time."

Robert let the rich brew warm his throat while he listened. Talking English classics was not his strong suit, but he understood struggling to pay college expenses. He had to work his classes around two jobs. "Your efforts are admirable," Robert said.

"Taking classes this way is not the way I'd

planned. I was scheduled to go full time ... but ... well, finances fell through."

A timer beeped, and Mary Sue pulled a casserole from the oven. Cheesy aroma wafted under his nose. "I understand you used to work for the state senator," Robert said.

"I suppose you heard that from Horace and Thelma Baxter." She cut into the casserole with a vengeance, distributed the plates and retrieved a basket of biscuits.

Robert glanced at Jane, showing off his manners by taking a biscuit and passing to the right. He pinched off a bite and buttered it. "Mmm." The biscuit was slightly crisp outside and fluffy on the inside. "Kitchen dining has its rewards. These biscuits are wonderful."

"I learned to make the biscuits from Mrs. Calhoun. The Baxters always requested them when they visited. They were nice enough to prepare for, but Mr. Berdanier and his cronies—I had no use for them."

"Why?" Jane asked.

"I used to be a part of the woodwork when the Calhouns entertained, and the men had their cigar smoking poker nights. But when Berdanier discovered I actually had goals and plans for college, that's when I got the ax."

"What happened?"

Mary Sue grabbed the coffee pot. "I was a hard worker. Mrs. Calhoun, Nadine, liked me. She fixed a room for me to stay rent free and I had my class schedule planned so that it didn't interfere with what she needed me to do." She refilled their cups including hers and placed the pot back on the warmer.

"One day Berdanier called me aside. I guess the Calhouns were too embarrassed to tell me." She sat down and wrapped her hands around her coffee up. "He said my services were no longer needed and gave me a final paycheck with an extra month's wages."

Her hands tightened on her cup. "Mr. Berdanier said, 'I hope you understand, but Mr. Calhoun is going to run for State Senator, and it might hurt him politically to have a single young woman living with him.' His implication was clear but Mr. Calhoun and I ... well you know. There was nothing romantic, but there was talk and ..."

"So, you had to change your college plans?"

"Yes. All because of ghastly rumors and Berdanier was the one fanning the flames. I can't afford rent and tuition to attend full time. So here I am. Taking one class at a time. It will take me awhile, but I'm determined." She smacked the table with her hand hard enough that it had to hurt, but she was on a roll. "And it galled me to have to serve that man again. Honestly, with his dealings it's no surprise someone took him out."

"Why do you say that?"

"Looking back, I think the real reason they got rid of me was that I heard more than they wanted. They had me fetching beer and snacks while they talked about different pet issues. At the luncheon Friday, I heard Miss Clark confront Berdanier about Roger Underwood and mineral rights. Mr. Underwood and Berdanier were thick and often came together."

"Who is this Underwood?"

"A businessman who deals in granite and other minerals. Since Mr. Calhoun became senator, he's sponsored legislation relaxing environmental restrictions, specifically providing for those with mineral leases to expand testing."

"Was Topazus ever mentioned for mineral exploration?" Robert asked.

"Not that I heard, but since Miss Clark mentioned an inquiry about Underwood from environmentalists, I'm guessing they could have been interested in this property."

The granite rock with one side polished sitting on Berdanier's desk and the rock Horace Baxter mentioned in the truth or lie game were clues, but how they tied together was not yet clear. "When business, laws, and politics become entangled, interesting alliances form."

Mary Sue sniffed. "And enemies."

~

Jane wiped her feet on the mat outside Berdanier's office. "Think of it. When Berdanier's ashes are scattered in the parking lot, he'll be going wherever people's feet take them. Weird."

"To Morgan City and beyond." Robert unlocked and pushed the door open. Jane stepped in and wrinkled her nose at the stale cigar smoke clinging to the air. Robert rolled up the window shades. A ray of light highlighted the phone on the desk.

Jane hung back. She hadn't called her brother.

Robert crossed the room and pulled the chain dangling under the globe of the vintage desk lamp which created another shaft of light on phone.

Cameo requested she contact her brother. *Call.*

"For a guy with uncouth manners, it's surprising that he had these antique pieces in his office." Robert said.

"Hmm ..." Uncouth might describe her. She'd been discourteous and ill-mannered to confront Adam when he was trying to help. Yet didn't psychology tout the need to be honest, straightforward, let people know how you feel, get feelings out in the open. That's what she had tried to do. Right?

But he clammed up. It was his turn to come out of his shell and face facts. Contacting him would give him that chance. He said his day off was Tuesday. Maybe he was on the other end of the phone trying to figure out a way to connect with her. *Call.*

Robert rapped on the credenza. "Earth to Jane."

She took her eyes off the phone.

Robert, head cocked at a tilt, stared at her. "You with me?"

She blinked. "Uh … sure."

"I was suggesting a plan for reviewing the files. You seem to be roaming in outer space."

"Sorry. It's my brother. I need to call him about the exterminator and roofer for Cameo and I'm dreading it."

"Why?"

"We parted on bitter terms yesterday and it's eating me."

"I thought you had reconnected and were getting along."

"We did, but I opened my big mouth and brought up his not coming to see Mother when she needed him."

"I imagine bringing up that raw subject wounds both of you."

"Yes. I'm trying to convince myself that I was right to confront him, but it doesn't feel right."

"If loving you is wrong, I don't want to be right?"

"Huh?"

He offered a slanted smile. "Old song."

"Oh."

"Having to call your brother again for assistance might put your relationship back on track." He peered over nonexistent glasses. "That is, if you can temper your inclination to fan the fire."

Was that what she was doing? Fanning a flame rather than clearing the air? Jane heaved a sigh, swallowed the sour taste in her mouth and reached for her phone.

Robert turned and started opening drawers on the credenza. "Don't over think it. I need your mind on the task at hand."

He was right. Too much thinking.

"Hello." Adam's voice seemed strained.

Stay upbeat. Don't mention the angry departure. "Cameo thanks you for helping with the mold and rat inspection. Do you know a roofer you'd recommend?"

"I do."

"Since you're off work today, any chance you could check on the electri—?"

"I … don't know, I have other commitments, but I'll call a roofer who is highly regarded."

"Thank you … I—" she looked at the phone screen. He'd hung up. Jane slipped her phone back into her purse.

"Back on track with your brother?"

"Not exactly …"

"Hello?" Jane looked up. A lady peered into the room. She had silver hair cut in a bob with a fringe of bangs and eyeglasses attached to a chain dangling about her neck.

"Yes?" Robert said.

"I saw the light and was curious to see who might be in here. I'm Sylvia Hangstrom from the antique shop next door."

"Robert Grey." He walked over and extended his hand. "This is my coworker Jane Carson. We're private investigators working to find information that might help in Mr. Berdanier's murder case."

"I understand Mrs. Clark at Topazus was arrested."

"Yes ma'am. But after the arrest is when our work to establish guilt or innocence begins."

"I see. Well, if I can be of any help. He was a good customer."

"I've been admiring his antique furnishings. Did he purchase them from you?" Jane asked.

She grinned and nodded. "The desk and credenza. Lovely Chippendale period pieces. Mint condition too."

"Did he purchase the wood file cabinets from you?" Robert asked

"No. He already had the cabinets." She walked over and ran her hand across a cabinet drawer. "Beautiful wood grain. Mr. Berdanier had a real appreciation for the fine workmanship of these vintage pieces." She turned around, shaking her head. "A tragedy him being killed at that plantation. There are some lovely antiques there. I was asked to price a fine Dresden mantle clock from Topazus a few days ago."

"Mr. Berdanier brought it in?"

"No. Not sure of his name. I've seen him around the jewelry store next door. I offered him three hundred dollars, but I think he may have been price shopping."

"Do you know what day it was?"

"Over the weekend. Saturday, I think. Yes ... it was the day poor Mr. Berdanier was murdered." Her head ticked from side to side. "Hard to imagine. Murdered." She made her way back to the door. "If there's any way I can help, I'll be next door."

Murder. The gravity of the word gripped Jane. Disagreement with her brother aside, she had a job to do and the task deserved her undivided attention.

~

Jane cringed when Robert leaned back in the office chair and propped his feet on the credenza.

"Careful." She grabbed a blank file folder. "Stick this under your feet."

"Antique stuff is way too delicate for my liking." Grumbling, he stuck the folder under his shoes. "How's that?"

She caught the gleam in his eye. "Better," she smirked.

"I believe I've found why Berdanier brought up heirs' property that rankled Katherine." Robert pulled a letter from a fat file. "A letter written to Micah Freedman and cc'd to Alfred Berdanier as trustee of Topazus estate from The Center for Heirs' Property Preservation. The correspondence is in answer to Micah's inquiry, and basically states that since early black landowners rarely made wills their descendants inherited the land without clear title. The center's mission is to assist legitimate heirs by having the land designated as heirs' property."

"If the deed we found is authentic, would that give Micah clear title?"

"Good question." Robert studied the paper a moment. "The designation is heirs, plural. Think of all the descendants that could be out there. I doubt Micah's the only one." Robert pulled the yellowed paper Jane discovered from his jacket pocket. "Finding heirs could complicate the purchase of the property and may be why Katherine didn't want Berdanier bringing it up."

"Frustrating for Micah."

"And a big legal hassle involving time and money that would kill the sale for Dean." Robert tucked the paper back in his jacket.

"Here's another interesting find." Pinching the corner of a paper, Robert held it up as though a tantalizing tidbit. "An interchange between Alfred Berdanier and Roger Underwood regarding mineral leasing requirements. They wanted Senator Calhoun to push for regulation changes that would bypass restrictions on land stripping."

"And from what Madison said, the land they wanted to strip was on the Topazus estate."

"Yup. Wheeling and dealing. No wonder Cameo was riled," Robert said. "Have you found anything of interest?"

Sitting on the desk's edge, Jane flipped to her notes.

"Whoa!"

Jane jumped, startled. "What?"

Robert stood and positioned the desk chair behind Jane. "The Chippendale desk might not be able to handle your weight."

Jane lifted her chin. "Thank you. I was testing you to see if you'd notice."

"Sure, you were," he snickered.

She stuck out her tongue.

"Rule number sixty-four. Never stick your tongue out at a fellow investigator."

"What about items ten through sixty-three?"

"I call 'em as I need 'em."

She plunked down on the chair. "Fine. I'll break 'em when needed." She squinted in his direction. "Back to what I've found." She held up her papers. "Being listed on the National Register is an honor but doesn't mandate preservation. If an owner doesn't value the property's history, the listing will not stop changes or demolition."

"Good news for Katherine and Dean if there is no preservation mandate."

"And I can see why Rita might want to cover the mold and other problems. Selling might look too attractive compared to the cost of repair," Jane said.

"Neglecting the building seems dumb when it would only deteriorate more and might not be repairable."

"Here's another item highlighted: preservation easement. It's a tool used to insure the preservation of the character-defining features of a property for the public's benefit. It's a likely point Berdanier had planned to share with Cameo."

"Hmm ... if an easement was approved, that could be a deal killer for Chandler by limiting their use of the property."

"And maybe why Berdanier would be interested. If he kept the status quo with an easement, he could pursue mineral exploration that would cease if the property sold to Chandler."

Robert sent her a genuine smile. "Your analysis has merit. Press on with the preservation material. I'll tackle the file cabinets."

After an hour, Robert whistled. Jane looked up from a listing of National Register benefits.

"What?"

He pulled a file from the bottom of a drawer labeled "archives" and brought it to the desk. "Look at this." She closed her folder, pushed it aside and Robert dropped the file folder in front of her. The tab read: Cathey, Sandra.

"My scalp prickled when I saw the name."

"Scalp prickled? What does that mean?"

He grasped the top of his head. "When my head prickles, I know I've discovered something significant."

"Women's intuition?"

"Uh ..." he scratched his head. "Since I'm of the male persuasion, I'd call it a red flag." Robert pulled up the chair from the credenza and sat beside her.

"At the luncheon Friday, Cameo turned the color of the fancy white tablecloth when Berdanier pitched this name."

Jane opened the file. Inside were news clippings encased in clear plastic.

The first article was dated December 21, 2002. Jane lifted it from the folder and read, "Car wreck claims life of teen. Sandra Cathey, 18, lost her life in a late-night single-car accident. The car she was driving belonged to Cameo Clark, granddaughter of Topazus owner, Stanford Clark." A sinking feeling struck her stomach. "Uh oh." She tilted her head toward Robert, then read the last line. "Circumstances surrounding the accident are under investigation."

Robert pulled out the next article. "This one is dated December 23, 2002. Is Teen's Death Vehicular Homicide? Circumstances surrounding the death of Sandra Cathey leave many unanswered questions. Witnesses at the party attended by the girls say that

Cameo Clark was behind the wheel of her sports car when she left the party. Parents of the teenager killed in the December 20 accident on Highway 378, question the facts surrounding their daughter's death. 'My daughter had gone to a Christmas party with Cameo Clark. Where was she at the time of the accident? Sandra didn't know how to drive a stick shift,' the victim's mother, Myra Cathey said. Clark claims that Sandra wanted to try driving the car and she let her. Her parents say their daughter would have never done that. They believe Cameo wrecked the car and tried to make it look like Sandra was driving."

"In January, it appears the situation was resolved," Jane said. She scanned the January 18, 2003 news story. "The parents protested but the death was ruled an accident and dismissed, not enough evidence."

Robert pulled out documents underneath the articles and examined them. "Oh, boy."

"What?"

"I am holding here some shrewd dealing by Alfred Berdanier's father, Mr. Torrance Berdanier, Esquire." He held the paper for Jane to see. "Stanford Clark, Cameo's grandfather signed over mineral rights to Torrance. The fine print states that Berdanier can manage the rights as he sees fit apart from the trust. Mineral rights revert back to Cameo Clark as beneficiary when the trust ends."

Wow. "Payoff for getting Cameo out of trouble? No wonder the interest in mineral leasing. Alfred Berdanier, as successor trustee, had control of the mineral rights."

"Exactly. And from what Mary Sue overheard at the senator's house, deals were discussed, and legislation passed regarding mineral exploration. If Berdanier had a deal going on the side…"

"Cameo would not be pleased." Jane aligned her eyes with Robert's.

He stood and raked his hands through his hair, letting them come to rest on back of his neck. "According to this stipulation, the way to stop Berdanier from making a deal would be to have him out of the picture. This bit of information gives Cameo motive, big time. Especially since she brought up getting a call about Roger Underwood."

Jane flipped to the back of the file. There was an envelope in the pocket of the folder. "What's this?" Jane pulled out the envelope. Inside was a handwritten note. She scanned to the bottom. Her stomach did a flip flop. It was signed by Cameo. Jane handed the note to Robert.

He frowned and read. "On December 20, 2002, I was driving on Highway 386 after attending a Christmas party. Sandra Cathey was with me. A deer jumped in front of the car. I swerved to miss it. The car left the road flipped and landed right side up. Sandra was flung from the car and killed. I was not drunk but I did drink alcohol at the party. I panicked, left her there and walked home I later stated that I had been teaching Sandra how to drive my car with a stick shift. She asked to drive my car, and I let her."

Robert carefully folded the note, placed it in the envelope and put it back in the file pocket. His jaw set and expression grim. "If this note is an accurate admission, Cameo is guilty of vehicular homicide."

CHAPTER TWELVE

"... but the case was dismissed." Jane rehashed the implications on their way back to Topazus. Cameo had called asking them to meet the roofer since Micah was tied up elsewhere and she was still in Granite Ridge.

"I've seen how these matters are rationalized. Cameo was eighteen, had college and a career ahead of her that could have been dashed had she been charged. There might have been leniency but drinking and leaving the scene of accident—she could have served time."

"And you say there's no statute of limitation on vehicular homicide."

"Yes. But reality is that it would be tough to bring a charge because all the evidence is gone."

Jane shook her head. "Still, Berdanier needled her about it."

"The more we dig, the deeper the issues."

"So, if they used a cover-up," Jane tapped her

index finger against her lips, "why would she let us plunder these files? Wouldn't she fear the discovery?"

"She was probably told the record of the incident had been destroyed, since the case was dismissed."

"But when Berdanier brought up Sandra Cathey ... was the mention of that name enough to make her want to rid the earth of him?"

Robert rubbed his forehead. "Finding out a person thought to be trustworthy is not, has been known to make people do crazy things."

Back at Topazus, Robert pulled in beside the van with the *Expert Roofing Contractors* sign on the side waiting on them. He punched in the gate key code provided to bed-and-breakfast guests, and they both drove to the house.

Riley Dinkins, who exhibited tattoo expressions of love for his mother on his right arm, and Emma on his left, introduced himself and pulled a ladder from his van.

Robert craned his neck watching Riley raise the ladder that clanged and rattled as it extended. "I guess you're accustomed to climbing that high?"

"Shoot, ain't nothin'. I've worked on twelve-story condos. Mind over matter. All you need are grippy bottom shoes and to tell yourself you're closer to the ground than an airplane."

"Ah." Robert pulled out his phone. "Could you take pictures of the roof and any damage while you're up there?"

"No problem. I can take pictures with my own phone and I'll add them to the report. You're welcome to come up and see firsthand."

"Appreciate the invite. But I'm not gifted with

mind over matter like you."

Riley grinned. "Gotcha." He climbed up the ladder as if it was kitchen step stool.

Jane and Robert walked back from the house to get a better view of Riley as he strolled with ease around the steep angled roof and took several pictures.

"I'm getting a sinking feeling in my stomach just watching him." Jane said. "Cleaning gutters on a flat roof is my speed."

"Heights, period, bother me." Robert still heard the screams, his own, as a six-year-old falling from the cliff in Pine Bluff where the big boys dove into the river. He grasped for anything to break his fall and came up with nothing. Hitting the water was like hitting a brick wall, knocking the breath out of him.

Since then, heights sent his nerve endings into a frenzy. Lori may have reconsidered taking him for better or worse if she'd known blowing leaves off the roof would end up her job. His contribution was holding the ladder, plugging in the extension cord, and looking like a wuss.

His phone sounded. Cameo.

"Dean has been released. His story didn't hold water," Cameo said.

"No surprise." He held the phone aside and told Jane the news. "What made them doubt his story?" Robert asked Cameo.

"He made a gasoline credit card purchase at a station thirty miles away from Topazus at the time of the murder and admitted to a false confession."

"Good police work."

"I'll be here with mother and meeting with her attorney. Did the roofer make it?"

"He's here now."

Robert ended the call and Jane asked. "Can Dean get in trouble for lying?"

"He could. But it's not likely under these circumstances. If he had sworn under oath in court it might be a different story."

Riley scrambled down the ladder. He opened the pictures he'd taken, and Robert and Jane looked on. "Bad shape," he said shaking his head and pointing to the overall shots of worn and chipped shingles. "There are squishy places. The roof needs to be replaced along with rebuilding the decking and sealing around chimneys." He pointed to close-up shots of deterioration. "There is bound to be serious water damage inside."

James pulled up in his Jaguar and got out.

"Hey," Riley said waving at James. "Been a long time. Remember me? Riley Dinkins."

James' forehead wrinkled and he issued a hesitant smile.

"Basketball. Ornery Coach Wilkins. Class of '98." Riley dropped hints.

"Uh … yes of course," James said. His eyes darted to Robert and then back to Riley. "It has been a long time."

"I've seen you on the Big M casino ship," Riley said. "But didn't want to interrupt your game. I sometimes go on weekends with the wife and—"

"Fancy that. Good to see." James clasped his hands and rubbed them together in jerky movements. "Sorry. I'm in a bit of a rush. I have to pick up something for my mother."

"Sure thing." Riley went to retrieve his ladder.

"I guess it was a relief to have your father released," Jane said.

"Yes. I told him it was a dumb thing to do." He tossed the remark over his shoulder, trotted up the front steps and disappeared inside.

Riley collapsed the extension ladder with a clang.

"Tell me about this casino ship. We might try it out," Robert said.

"The ship docks in Myrtle Beach and sails far enough off the coast to gamble legally seven days a week. You can play roulette, poker and blackjack. But me and the wife stick to the slots. We decide how much we can lose, then enjoy the food and the view."

"Sounds sensible. Does James play the slots too?"

"No. I see him at the craps tables. He's a platinum card holder. Those guys get drinks and food brought to them." He heaved the ladder into the back of the van. "Too rich for me."

James came out of the house and hurried to his car, not bothering to speak to them again.

"Busy man," Riley said, shaking his head and watching the Jaguar pull away. "And a good basketball player." He reached in his front pocket and handed his business card to Robert. "I'll work up the numbers as best I can and be in touch. Some things I can't predict until I tear into the roof and see how much damage is underneath."

"Thank you for coming," Jane said. "My brother spoke highly of you."

"Adam's your brother? Salt of the earth. When Adam tells you something you can take it to the bank." Riley climbed in his van and waved good-bye.

"Strange," Robert said. "You'd think James would

have at least inquired about the roof."

"Maybe he's on information overload with his father's confession and legal issues." Jane plunked down on the front steps. "I'm on overload myself assimilating information about historic preservation, property inheritance, mineral rights—"

"And vehicular homicide." Robert sat beside her, elbows propped on thighs, chin resting on clasped hands. "Some vacation."

"Call me crazy but it is disconcerting to hear my brother's word is so respected when I couldn't count on him." Jane tugged a strand of straightened hair behind her ear, picked up a leaf from the step and let it flutter to the ground.

"Hopefully, you can clear the air with him." Robert's phone sounded and Cameo's name appeared on the screen. "Our employer again." He answered and touched speaker phone symbol.

"Mom and I are on the way. Meet us at Crest Manor in a few. I've got pizza."

~

Over pizza and soft drinks at the dining table, they discussed the roofer's findings and Cameo filled them in on the morning's events.

"James was really upset with his dad."

"I bet," Robert said, taking a bite of cheesy goodness.

"He should have been. So was I." Katherine said. "I know he wants to help but—"

"But that was a stupid stunt, confessing to the murder," Cameo said. She tore off a piece of pizza with a vengeance. "It muddies the water and throws more suspicion on you."

"I think he sees that now," Katherine said. "He looked pitiful when he left and now he has to square things at his workplace."

Robert hoped to bring the conversation back in focus. "You said you met with the lawyer. Where do things stand right now?"

"Next is plea date and then a date will be set for the preliminary hearing. Jennings wants follow-up interviews with all witnesses that law enforcement took statements from. Since you're here Robert, he is fine with using you instead of his investigator." Cameo handed him a folder. "These are your copies of the interviews. As for me, I'm interested in learning more on Berdanier. Were you able to find anything beneficial in his office?"

"We did." Robert retrieved his briefcase where he had stashed the paperwork for Cameo to see.

Jane squirmed in her seat. "All I could think of when we arrived there was that one day, we might be tracking through Alfred Berdanier's cremains."

"We may never truly be rid of him." Cameo's remark was blunt.

Robert pulled papers and the lid dropped shut with a *thud*. "Say that again."

"About never being rid of him?" Cameo asked.

"No. Jane, about tracking his remains."

She cocked her head. "When you walk through the law office parking lot, you could get Berdanier's ashes on your shoes?"

"Katherine, are those ashes that spilled from the grill still outside?" Robert asked.

"I suppose so. I put the grill back together, but the ashes are still scattered. Why?"

"Do you have a plastic bag and spoon. I need to take a sample."

The smoky smell of charcoal ash mixed with sticky grilled steak juices lingered near the grill on the patio. There had been no rain since Friday, so the ashes remained light and powdery.

"Is your head prickling?" Jane knelt beside him and spoke softly. Robert nodded as he gathered a sample with the plastic spoon and baggie that Katherine had provided. "I'll explain later," he whispered.

"There." He stood, sealing the bag. "That should be a good sampling. It may prove nothing. But since you said your gun was beside the overturned grill before you moved it to the back porch, the ashes may be of some value."

Cameo frowned and shrugged. "You're the investigator."

The investigator. He was Hale's *Man Without a Country*. Jane would be impressed that he was aware of the classic. In his case he was an investigator without a department.

He had no authority and no access to evidence analysis. It was demoralizing to no longer be on top and in control. He'd have to send the sample to his agent friend and depend on his benevolence.

When reassembled inside, Robert placed the packaged ashes in his briefcase. "Sorry for the interruption." He pulled out paperwork gleaned from Berdanier's office. "I know you're interested in the information we found today. Jane, go first with historical preservation."

Jane took the file Robert handed her and flipped it open. "Topazus was placed on the National Register in

1974. Since Chandler Development was interested in the property, Berdanier was evidently checking to see if there were restrictions related to the historical designation."

Katherine huffed. "How can you be made to —"

Cameo held her palm up to her mother. "Let her finish."

Katherine sucked in a deep breath, its release loud, but she remained quiet.

"This should put you at ease.," Jane said. "A listing on the National Register is considered an honor but does not carry restrictions on the property owner or mandate preservation."

"That's a relief." Katherine crossed her arms and leaned back in her chair.

"Berdanier did highlight a section encouraging property owners who were interested in long-term preservation to explore a tool called preservation easements. A portion of property is set aside as an easement for the public's benefit. Also, in his file are references to grants that can be obtained to restore old buildings."

"*Bah*. Good money after bad." Katherine pushed back from the table. "Anyone want coffee?" Robert nodded along with Jane.

"Good idea, Mom," Cameo drummed the table with her fingers. "Historical agencies may provide tools to restore, but with this roof report, repairs could be extensive. She frowned and shook her head.

"The house having serious problems doesn't surprise me." Katherine said, pulling coffee from the cupboard. "Rita wants to run the house and reign as mistress and have nothing interfere, including mold and mildew"

"Rita did receive a good mold report," Cameo said.

"Ordered and paid for by her." Spoons and cups clanked, and the cupboard doors banged as Katherine put the coffee on and talked. "Rita hoped to show there was no reason to consider the development plan that Dean presented. She has put her head in the sand and thinks Topazus is fine because she *wants* it to be fine."

"It's interesting that Berdanier invited Dean to the luncheon to discuss the developer's proposal." Robert said.

"And that probably scared Rita witless." Katherine set a tray on the counter with a *clunk*. "She needs Topazus for her catering business. If the place sold, she'd be out of luck. "

The coffee timer beeped. Cameo went to the kitchen and retrieved the coffee pot while Katherine carried the tray with cups and coffee extras to the table.

"Besides Rita's wishful thinking, I'd like to know how the deterioration got so out of hand," Cameo said.

"Mismanagement by the trustee." The cups rattled as Katherine deposited the tray on the table. "You reap what you sow. Berdanier needed to go."

Cameo's brow creased.

Robert scrutinized Cameo's reaction. She wasn't her mother's lawyer and he was not working the case for the state, but that kind of remark didn't help Katherine's defense.

Cameo poured coffee for everyone. "Sowing and reaping. Micah has hopes for a good cotton crop this next year."

Katherine let out a strangled sound as she sipped her coffee. "But what about the next flood or hurricane?"

Cameo's shift in subject did nothing to deescalate the conversation and Robert's news wasn't going to help, but it had to come out sometime. "Speaking of Micah I have heirs' property information." Robert pulled the yellowed document from his jacket. "Jane found this paper tucked in the pages of a ledger while exploring in the library." He handed Cameo the paper.

She stared at the document. Her mother slipped on reading glasses and read over her shoulder.

Katherine's jaw visibly tensed. She returned to her seat. "Heirs' property." She spat out the words. "Berdanier stirring things up."

"Berdanier can't be blamed for this," Cameo said. "Micah said he was told that property had been deeded to his ancestors, but he never had proof. This looks genuine. What book was this in?"

"A ledger on a shelf near the fireplace."

Cameo nodded. "It's signed by Morgan Danford Clark. She held her hand over the document, lightly touching the signature. Daddy said he freed his slaves before the Civil War. Micah's ancestors elected to stay, and his family members have always been provided a home and land for their personal use."

"And they should be," Katherine said. "But the legalities ... don't you see? Berdanier was manipulating us like puppets."

Katherine had a point. Did Berdanier have a copy of this deed? Had the deed been hidden from Micah's ancestors, preventing its being filed? Was Berdanier the proverbial snake in the grass lying in wait for his opportunity to use the information for his own benefit?

"Berdanier's file on heirs' property references the

fact that tracing down ownership when heirs' property is involved complicates land purchases," Robert said. "It might pose more trouble than the developer would want to take on."

"My point exactly." Katherine popped the table. "Berdanier was a menace."

Cameo pressed steepled fingers to her lips. "Micah might have thought all his faithful years on the estate would count for nothing. If the land was sold to developers, there'd be no more cotton crop and no more need of him."

"Could he have felt he was in a desperate situation?" Jane tossed in the question and Robert followed up, "And shot Berdanier to stop sale of the land and protect his job?"

Katherine brows pushed together, and Cameo shook her head.

Jane's phone beeped and she checked it. "Sorry. A text to call the guy who made the rat and mold inspection." She excused herself to make the call outside.

Robert forged ahead. "While on difficult topics, there is one more item I uncovered related to mineral rights and the name Berdanier brought up on Friday."

"What name?" Katherine asked.

"Sandra Cathey."

Cameo froze. She held her coffee cup mid-air then slowly returned it to the saucer with a clink. The tendons on Katherine's neck tightened.

Robert slid the file in front of Cameo. "I found this folder stashed in back of one of the file cabinets."

Cameo touched the name on the top of the folder and slowly opened it. Her chin quivered and her fingers visibly trembled.

He might as well press on with what he knew. Rip the bandage off quickly; there was no point in letting the pain linger. "At the time of this incident, Torrance Berdanier was given Topazus estate mineral rights over the course of the trust. Alfred Berdanier, as successor, was looking into mineral leasing. But the rights were to revert back to the estate when the trust ended—"

Katherine held up both hands and slapped them to the table. "Stop." The word shot out like a bullet. "You needn't speculate further. I killed Berdanier."

CHAPTER THIRTEEN

The cool air outside Crest Manor refreshed Jane while she spoke to Butch Anderson. After ending the call, she remained outside to take in the view from the hill. The Topazus mansion stood proud, masking the problems inside.

Butch had said he could rid the house of rats but repeated his recommendation to wait on the roof and leak repairs. "Call me back when you're ready for me or have Adam call. See what your brother thinks. He's a guy you can depend on, but I guess you know that. I'd trust his opinion."

But I guess you know that. Jane puzzled over the way her brother was perceived by those he worked with. He had been the guy she could depend on as a youngster too. But where was he during their mother's illness? He had never given her an explanation.

She rolled back her shoulders and took in another deep breath before returning to the porch. She stepped into the kitchen and raised voices.

"What are you saying?" Cameo shrieked at her mother. She leaned in a half standing position against the table, her hair falling forward.

Jane took a step back. What was going on?

Katherine sat at the table, eyes closed, hands clenched beneath her chin, tearful.

Cameo pushed herself upright. "Don't. Do. This." Her words were commanding and precise.

Katherine opened her eyes. The silver strip of her hair highlighted the piercing stare she fixed on Cameo. She spoke with equal, measured force. "You heard me. I killed Berdanier. I thought I could get away with it. But I can't let this go any further."

Jane gawked; her feet frozen to the kitchen floor. Robert still sat at the table. What must he be thinking?

"Berdanier could not be trusted." Katherine's eyebrows pulled into a deep crease. "He needed to go."

"But ..." Cameo grabbed the hair that had fallen over her eye and yanked it behind her ear. "You're lying."

Jane attempted to absorb the scene playing out in front of her. Katherine admits she shot Berdanier?

Katherine straightened in her chair and wiped at a tear. "When I heard you got a call from environmental people about Underwood, I knew Berdanier must be working a deal. The threat of heirs' property was bad enough." She jerked up her chin. "Chandler wouldn't want land with separate mineral rights."

Cameo continued shaking her head. "No. I don't believe you."

"You better believe me and get used to it." Katherine's words were sharp.

Cameo jabbed an accusing finger at her mother.

"You left the luncheon, grabbed your gun, ran and waited at the front gate for Berdanier to leave, shot him, returned to the house and put the gun back and then took a stroll?" Cameo banged her fist on the table making the coffee cups jump. "You forget, I saw you returning from the river."

"I didn't run to the gate. I took the cart." Katherine leveled hard eyes on Cameo. "You forget, I've already been arrested."

Jane propped herself against the counter, weak-kneed.

Robert's phone buzzed, cracking the mother-daughter stand-off that had turned into glares of defiance.

"It's Micah," he told Cameo.

"See what he wants but wait on telling him about the deed. I need to research it." Cameo reverted to issuing orders.

Robert joined Jane in the kitchen. With Micah still on the phone, he gave her elbow a squeeze and steered her toward the door.

"How can she be thinking about deeds when her mother just confessed to murder?" Jane whispered.

He shielded the phone. "Because Cameo is rattled. The Cathey issue and mineral rights make Cameo a solid suspect."

~

"She's right here." Robert handed Jane the phone.

"Can you please see if your brother can come?" Micah asked. "He understands our electrical situation here. I just discovered the refrigerator has been off for some time."

"I'll see what I can do," Jane said.

"The power in the Topazus kitchen is out." Jane handed Robert's phone to him and reached in her purse for her phone. "He wants me to contact Adam."

"Okay. Call your brother." Robert touched her back, steering her in the direction of the front drive where he had parked. "We'll see if we can be any help to Micah and leave Cameo here to hash things out with her mother."

"This place has turned into a circus," Jane said hurrying with Robert to his truck.

"With seven rings instead of three." Robert opened her door.

"Seven?"

"Seven suspects." He closed her door and Jane scrolled for Adam's number. "I told Adam there were more electrical issues this morning, but he cut me off."

"Won't hurt to try him again."

Adam's abrupt end to their phone conversation this morning was likely his way of avoiding her after their argument. Still, he knew how bad the electrical problems were at Topazus. With the rosy light his coworkers saw him in, maybe he'd make time to help.

When they reached the Topazus kitchen, Micah had the refrigerator pulled from the wall. Jane listened as he explained the problem to Robert, while waiting for the call to Adam to connect. The signal for her cell phone had been erratic on Topazus property.

"I wanted to talk to you," Micah told Robert, "but it will wait. "Items in the freezer are starting to thaw. I replaced the fuse, but it kicked off after a few seconds. It's either this outlet or the plug." Micah grabbed a screwdriver and slid behind the refrigerator.

"What are you going to do?" Robert asked.

"Take this outlet cover off."

Jane's call screen finally lit up. Bethany answered. Maybe she could convince Adam to come even if he wouldn't come for Jane. "Bethany, since it's Adam's day off, he is really needed at Topazus. He cut me off earlier—"

As Jane spoke, there was a buzzing sound followed by a crackle. Sparks flew. A flame shot out from behind the refrigerator. Micah's body jerked in spasms, knocking between the refrigerator and the wall.

"Oh my God!" Jane cried out.

"Micah!" Robert tugged the refrigerator further out. Micah slumped to the floor. Pungent burnt electrical smell permeated the air.

Bethany's voice startled. "Jane? Jane, what's wrong?"

"Sparks … flames ..." The words stuck in her throat.

Robert knelt beside Micah, his hand pressed against his neck. "He has an erratic heartbeat. I'm calling 911."

"Jane. Talk to me what's happening?" Bethany called out over the phone.

"It's Micah." Jane's lips trembled. "I think he's been electrocuted."

Jane heard muffled talking and then Bethany said, "Adam will send someone to Topazus."

"Why doesn't *he* come?" A hardness hit Jane's stomach. Micah was worried about the refrigerator one minute, then on the floor motionless the next. Life was so fragile. The flash of fire and sparks had left her with spots before her eyes. "He ... tell him to forget it now. It's too late." The words tumbled out. She'd spoken the same words when Adam said he'd come to their mother's funeral.

"Jane don't worry your brother," Robert said. "Medical help is on the way. Find a blanket. Micah's unconscious."

~

By the time emergency arrived, Robert had notified Cameo, and she in turn had reached Micah's wife, Inez.

Jane stood back with Robert, Cameo, and Katherine to let EMTs do their work. Inez knelt near Micah.

When Micah's eyes blinked open, Jane's "Thank you. Lord," slipped out on whispered breath.

Dazed, Micah asked what had happened.

"You were shocked by some faulty wiring, honey." Inez said. The EMTs checked his vitals, attached a cardiac monitor, and administered oxygen before lifting him onto a stretcher and loading him into the ambulance.

"Inez ride with me," Cameo said. "We'll follow him to the hospital."

"Please, call me when you know more about his condition," Katherine said and left on the Crest Manor cart.

Outside the kitchen, Jane shook her head and watched the ambulance followed by Cameo leave. Her arms wrapped tight around her, she shivered against the cold. "If my brother had come, none of this would have happened."

"You cannot blame your brother for this," Robert pulled off his jacket and draped it on her shoulders.

She tugged the arms of the jacket close. "Thank you." She sniffed and he handed her his handkerchief.

She must look awful, which was how she felt. "This was Adam's day off. He knew how bad the electric wiring was and now this."

"If he had the day off, he must have had other plans."

"He saw the call was from me and had his wife answer." She kicked at the ground. "You know how that goes."

"He came Saturday when you called, brought his children Sunday, and he made arrangements for the exterminator and roofer. Don't you think you should give him some slack?"

"Sure." Her smile bitter. "I should have known. Not coming when it's critical is his way. I needed him desperately when Mom and Dad split up. And when mother was dying, I needed him more than ever and he didn't come. Seeing Micah laying there so helpless ..." Tears trickled down her cheeks and she swiped at them.

Robert placed his hands on her shoulders. "Micah, unconscious, brought all the hurt back. Sit down." He pointed to a bench beside the herb garden.

His voice was low and filled with concern, confounding her. He held her eyes with a steady gaze. Her face felt hot. She blew her runny nose.

"It's hard to let go of old resentment. Trust me. I know from the grudge I held against Eckstrand when he jumped on the theft case against me. It was hard but I had to accept blame for my actions."

"But you were falsely charged—and Eckstrand apologized."

"I looked guilty and Eckstrand was doing his job. I shouldn't have hung blame on him. Did your brother promise to come today?"

Jane sighed. "No. I see where you're headed with this lecture." She flicked at a piece of lint on her slacks. "But I thought he would and as it turned out he should have."

"If the old adage is correct, your living with resentment and reminding Adam he did wrong is like stirring a teaspoon of arsenic into your coffee every morning, hoping it will hurt Adam."

Jane tensed. What her brother did was wrong. Period. She had sacrificed her own peace to make sure he knew he had hurt her. He needed to know. Didn't he? He needed to … what? She didn't know what.

"Think about it. Your resentment hasn't changed *him* or what happened. It's changed *you*."

His eyes latched onto hers. She shifted on the hard bench, gathered her hair over one shoulder and dropped her gaze to her hands, clasping them tight.

"It's hurt you." He tapped her knee. "Your anger is based on the distorted belief that he should have done what *you* wanted. Unless you've learned some way to change the past, the past is as good as it's going to get. You don't have to like the past to accept it. That fact alone is what freed me from anger and resentment. My instincts tell me your brother needs a second chance. We all do."

Jane blew out tense air. His words struck smack in the middle of the wound she'd latched onto. Was it possible to turn loose of her bitterness? Could she give him a second chance? She jiggled her hands to revive the circulation. "When did you get to be so smart?"

"Beats me. You bring out the philosopher in me." He patted her on the shoulder. "Better now?"

"I … maybe." Like a loose strand on a ball of

twine, she'd reel in her emotion and tuck it away for now. "Mentally, I see your point. I can't change the past. But—"

Robert held up his hand. "Let it settle. Micah is in good hands. Your brother is not at fault. Put your mind on something else. Help me glean evidence from ashes."

She pushed her hair from her face. "What is the sudden interest in ashes anyhow?"

"After leaving the crime scene the day Berdanier was killed, I drove one of the carts back and later noticed ashes and soot on my shoes. I thought it came from the bonfire but when I saw the ashes at Crest Manor ... whoever picked up the gun had to walk through them."

"Ah ... And you think if the sooty residue on your shoes came from Crest Manor ... then ... then how did they get in the cart?"

"My theory. The murderer got ashes on his or her shoes when he took the gun, and then on the foot pedals in the cart which then transferred to my shoes when I drove the cart."

"So, if the ash on your shoes are from Crest Manor, how do you figure out who tracked the stuff?"

"Follow me."

Jane walked behind him to the rear kitchen entry.

"All participants at the luncheon heard about the gun and where it was kept," Robert said as he climbed the steps to the service porch.

"What do you hope to find here?"

"When I met you on these back steps to tell you about the search warrant after the tea on Saturday, I noticed the slip-on garden shoes had a dusting of gray residue on them which could have come from the bonfire. But the sooty stuff could also have come from the spilled ashes at Crest Manor."

Jane scrutinized the soft pliable shoes. "If the murderer had on dress shoes and wanted to steal away to Crest Manor and the woods, they might use the garden shoes?"

"Precisely. And there was opportunity. Everyone scattered after the luncheon." Robert picked up the garden shoes. His brows lifted. "Yup. Ashes and soot streaks. Just like those on my shoes. See if you can find a plastic spoon and storage bags."

Jane found the items in the kitchen drawer beside the sink and retrieved a marking pen from Rita's desk. Robert scraped a sample from the shoes into the bag. "Now for the carts," he said.

Outside, two Topazus carts sat next to the kitchen service entrance.

"You drove the one with the reindeer ornament hanging on the mirror." Jane walked behind the carts. "They have number one and two mini-plates. Number one is the cart you drove."

"Good. Label the scrapings accordingly, and we'll take a stroll up the hill to collect a sample from the cart that Katherine drives."

"Then what?"

"Fortunately, I've been wearing casual shoes and never cleaned the mess off my dress shoes. I'll take a scraping from them and overnight all the ash samples to Agent Freed for analysis."

Jane held the bags for Robert and watched him work. Her mind drifted in the silence to Micah slumped on the kitchen floor. "Robert, we all teeter on a fine line between life and death."

"Now you're the philosopher?"

"Think about it. Sandra Cathey was a young girl having fun with a friend. Laughing one minute, gone the next. Micah was conducting a simple task and now is struggling back from a brush with death. Berdanier was relishing his cheesecake one moment and then he was shoved into eternity before he could digest his dessert."

Robert handed her a bag of gray powder to label. She held it up. "The stuff we come from and return to. The idea sent goosebumps running up her arms.

CHAPTER FOURTEEN

Robert rubbed his cold hands together. Being in a hospital again, more than the temperature, chilled him. He and Jane stepped from the elevator onto the third floor in search of Micah's room.

Subdued lighting, polished floors, echoes of food trays gathered on rumbling metal carts, smells of alcohol and disinfectant—the backdrop of his last days with his wife. Her hand had grasped his, then her grip slowly released, and a vibrant, gifted life slipped away, leaving him hollow and numb. She'd been gone two years, but the reminders stung.

"Here it is," Jane said. "Room 342."

Robert tapped on the partially open door. Inez, with less stress in her brown eyes than yesterday, appeared at the door and pushed it open for them to come in. "Micah, you have company."

Inside, a boy and girl in their early teens looked up from tablets. Micah was sitting up in bed. "Kids, these are the two who witnessed my pyrotechnic display."

"A scary stunt you better not repeat." Inez scolded, then introduced the children, Emma and Casey,

"How are you?" Robert asked Micah.

"Okay, I guess." He wore an oxygen cannula in his nose, had fluids running into one arm, and a blood pressure cuff on the other.

"The doctor said he should rest a couple of days." Inez said. She snugged her arms about her, casting a look of concern. "He lost some function in his right arm."

"But I'm gradually getting back some feeling." Micah said, pumping his hand.

"I see you've been dining on good old hospital food." The remains of tea, a Popsicle stick, mashed potatoes and meat loaf sat on a tray beside the bed. "Have you and the children had lunch yet?" Robert asked Inez.

"I've been trying to get them to go get something to eat," Micah said.

"Not and leave you alone."

"Why not take a break while we're here?"

The mention of food produced smiles from Casey and Emma. "We're famished, Mom."

"You don't mind?"

"No. Take your time."

The threesome left, promising to bring Micah the cheeseburger he'd been craving.

Robert and Jane took seats. "Were you able to sleep last night?" Jane asked.

If Robert were asked that question, he would have to say, "little to none." After overnighting the ash samples, he and Jane had pored over the interviews and police reports in the discovery material Cameo had provided.

Micah's answer was, "Sporadic. Nurses and techs kept me up taking my temperature, administering breathing treatments, and taking blood. If the doctor wants me to rest, I'll have to go home."

Robert smiled. "Understood. You picked a tough way to get out of work."

"That's what I get for impatience. I've learned my lesson about messing with electricity. From now on, I'm leaving it to the experts."

"I'm sorry Adam didn't make it," Jane said. "I had thought he would. But—"

Robert cut off her guilt trail. "You called me yesterday, Micah. Was there something else you needed to talk about before all the electrical excitement?"

His forehead wrinkled, and he blinked. "After getting zapped, I totally forgot. There was something. Maybe it will come to me."

"I've been reading over the statements taken by the police after Berdanier's murder. Are you up to answering a few questions?"

Micah frowned, then shrugged. "I suppose so."

"Beside the back door of the kitchen, I noticed a pair of clog type garden shoes. Who do those belong to?"

"I purchased them for Rita, Mary Sue or me to slip on when it's messy outside. We use them when gathering flowers or vegetables from the garden to keep from messing up our shoes or tracking in."

"Tell me about Rita's hosting. How long has she played the part of Martha Lee Clark?"

"As long as I can remember. My dad said that Lela, that's Cameo's grandmother who was losing her health, insisted Rita take over the role."

"I understand Rita and Cameo's father were an item in high school until Katherine moved here and stole his heart," Jane said.

"That was before my time, but according to my father, Lela and Stanford were set on Rita being their daughter-in-law. Lela even allowed Rita to wear the Topazus ring during special events. It shocked the family when Morgan eloped with Katherine after he graduated from law school. When he moved to Alabama and didn't return to Topazus, Katherine was blamed."

"Do you think that is why the trust was established?"

"I've been told that the negative stance of the senior Clarks was because Katherine never appreciated the traditions and legacy of Topazus. Rita has always encouraged James' and Cameo's relationship over the years. She said it would put the lineage straight."

"But if Katherine was a Belle, she must have appreciated the home and its history," Jane said.

Micah shrugged. "She was only involved her senior year in high school and didn't have as much time invested in Topazus as Rita. I believe Rita wants Topazus to remain the same and has trouble facing the reality of its decline. The mansion can't sit pristine and lovely forever."

"Yet with all that negativity, Katherine lives on the property." Robert said.

"When Morgan retired, Katherine didn't want to live in the house. I don't blame her. Rita operated a lot of her catering business from the house and was running the show."

"Were you surprised Katherine was arrested for shooting Berdanier?"

"Very. Unless it was her way of finally getting revenge for being cut off by the trust. But I don't see her being that passionate about it to kill."

"Where does Dean fit in?" Jane asked.

Micah slowly shook his head from side to side. "Always on the fringes. Rita married Dean after Morgan married Katherine, but they divorced when James was still young."

"Do you know how he became involved in this offer to buy Topazus?"

Micah balled his good hand into a fist. "All I know is he has a real estate office close by and was retained as a local rep for the development company."

"Do you know anything about James and gambling?" Robert asked.

Micah's brow creased. "He's mentioned going to Myrtle Beach on the weekends. There's a casino ship that docks there. But I don't know if he gambles or not."

"You showed the exterminator hidden spaces," Jane said. "Are there other secret places in the house?"

A good question and Robert liked the way she posed it. He wanted to probe deeper into Micah's knowledge of the goings on around the estate. Having Jane along might make the questions less intimidating.

"Uh ... well ... no. No, not that I know of."

"What do you think of the developer's offer to purchase the estate in light of the declining condition of the mansion and finances?" Jane asked.

A good lead-in for his bulls-eye question.

"I'm not sure what the offer is exactly, but it

sounds as though they would handle preserving the home and the church."

"What would happen to you and your employment?" Robert asked.

Micah lost eye contact and the pitch of his voice rose. "I don't know what it would mean. The cotton crop has sustained the estate all these years but was hit hard with the recent weather disasters. I told Berdanier it looked like we'd have a good crop this year to put us in the black."

"But it sounded like he was considering other financial avenues."

"Maybe" Micah shifted in the bed and tugged at the oxygen line resting over his ears.

"Cameo mentioned a mineral lease. Do you know anything about that?"

"Not for certain ... this is rumor... but I understand mineral rights were given to Alfred Berdanier's father. Mr. Berdanier senior talked a lot to my dad about the rock formations on the farm. Said there could be more value sitting under the ground than on top."

"Do you know what he meant?"

"Granite." A flush crept up Micah's throat. "But have you seen the results of digging a quarry? Huge trucks trounce the ground." Micah's good hand grasped a wad of sheet at his side. "Machines gouge the earth and strip the soil, creating a wasteland. I thought Berdanier had settled on sticking with the cotton crop, but ... well ... it's up to Cameo to decide now."

"We're back." Inez entered with the children, carrying fast food sacks. "The machine blinked Micah's latest blood pressure reading as 170 over 100.

Inez frowned at Micah and then Robert. "Whatever

you're discussing has sent his blood pressure up."

"Sorry," Robert said. "We don't want you to overdo, Micah. Thank you for talking to us."

Jane move to the door and Robert followed. "Cameo sends her best and will come to see you after dealing with legal issues regarding her mother's arrest."

He left off the part about Katherine's confession and still wondered what Micah had wanted to discuss but couldn't remember.

Leaving the hospital, Robert saw a familiar face coming from a separate building. "Isn't that—"

"My brother," Jane said under her breath. "Adam, Bethany," Jane called to them. "What are you doing here?"

"I uh ... I was just going to call you," Adam said. "I sent someone to Topazus. The wiring in the kitchen is repaired. But just like I said, the wiring is old and really should be replaced all over the house." Adam was pale. He edged over to a lamppost, leaned against it, and forced a smile.

Adam's wife raised her head and crossed her arms. "Either you tell her, or I will."

Adam closed his eyes and shook his head slowly.

"Tell me what?" Jane asked.

"I'm on kidney dialysis."

~

Jane had awakened early and couldn't go back to sleep. Her brother's admission and her own insensitivity nagged her. The scripture, "be still and know that I am God," had sent her to the gazebo in the garden as the perfect place to be still.

She gazed above the tree line at pink and orange streaked clouds showcased against the winter sky.

There was something cathartic in a sunrise. The display provided a daily reminder of God's creation and a visible way to feel his presence.

Jane rubbed her hands against her upper arms. Clear vinyl inserts lined the gazebo, creating walls to ward off the cold. But her chill came from inside. She'd been quick to judge her brother. Why hadn't she considered there might be a reason that prevented him from coming to their mother's side? Had she created such a formidable wall that prevented him from telling her about his problems? There she went again, second guessing his motives for not telling her about his illness. She'd even blamed Adam for Micah's getting hurt.

Footsteps sounded outside. Robert pushed back the vinyl flap and poked his head in. "Trouble sleeping?"

Jane nodded. Tears pressed.

"I thought I might find you here."

The understanding tone in his voice brought on the waterworks. She buried her head in her hands, her hair falling forward.

"Hey." She felt his arms encircle her. Their warmth soothing. Her body shuddered against his. He patted her back. "I didn't mean to upset you."

"No. It's not you." She sniffed and pulled away from his shoulder. "It's me. I feel awful for the hard feelings I had toward Adam. All I thought about was me." Jane brushed away the tears and tried to straighten her hair.

"Your emotions were raw, losing your mother."

"I let my brother down." Pain struck in the back of her throat. "Adam told me that since I had just quit my job to care for our mother, he didn't want to add to my concerns by telling me about his kidney disease." She wrung her hands. "I made him feel that he couldn't tell me."

Robert gave a single nod. "Just as I thought." His lips morphed into a grin, "You are putting on a cloak of guilt, but that will render you useless physically and mentally." He pushed back a stray strand of hair hanging over her eye. "I'm here to help however I can."

Jane raised her eyes heavenward, blinking back the tears. "I don't want to be useless." Jane studied Robert's eyes and drank in the sincere concern. "Not mentally. Not physically… physically …that's it."

She stood and grabbed Robert's hands. He was a direct conduit streaming into her spirit, confirming what she should do. "It's me that needs the second chance. I want to be evaluated for a kidney transplant."

Robert gave a light nod. His eyes warmed, squeezing her heart. "Let's find out what the procedure is."

~

Relief flooded Robert. Jane's countenance had changed since she talked to Bethany and made an appointment for a transplant evaluation.

"What are the chances you're a good match?"

"Bethany says statistically, being related increases my chances by 25%." Before taking a breath, Jane's words spilled out. "But if I am a match, I'll be out of commission awhile and—"

"Whoa. One thing at a time. You're here with me now, which I appreciate. You have an appointment after Christmas to see if you can help your brother. And you need to stay healthy, so let's eat." Robert opened the back door to the Topazus central hall and mouthwatering smells escaped.

Inside, Rita carried a silver covered dish to the dining table set for two. "Good morning. It's only you two today. Cameo joined James in Granite Ridge for breakfast."

Rita set the casserole on the table, lifted the lid, and a delicious aroma wafted out. "Topazus signature garden quiche, blueberry muffins, and poached pears with cream will round out the breakfast fare this morning. I hope Mary Sue took good care of you on Tuesday."

"She catered to our requests perfectly." Robert didn't mention that Mary Sue let them eat in the comfort of the kitchen.

"I gave Mary Sue the day off. She plans to see the Calhouns that she used to work for before Mr. Calhoun became a senator." Rita poured coffee. "I hope it's just a friendly visit. She's a reliable worker, and I wouldn't want to lose her."

Had a door opened for Mary Sue to get her old job back now that Berdanier was out of the way? Robert tucked that information away.

"Everything looks and smells wonderful," Jane said. "Please join us."

"I believe I will. It does my heart good to know that James and Cameo are managing some time alone. Those two are made for each other, don't you think?"

Robert took note of her comment in relation to what Micah had said about putting the lineage straight. "They certainly have a lot in common," Robert said.

Rita pulled items for another place setting from the buffet and poured coffee for herself. "I don't normally sit with the guests, but I do want to thank you for helping avoid disaster when Micah was hurt."

"I'm glad we were there to make the 911 call," Robert said.

"Watching sparks fly and Micah fall to the floor was horrifying," Jane said.

"I was in Granite Ridge with a bridal luncheon and came as soon as I received word from Cameo about the accident." Rita cut into the quiche and held her hand out for Jane's plate. She served Jane, Robert, and then herself. "The technician your brother sent couldn't have been nicer and had things working in no time."

"Micah deserves credit for discovering the power outage." Robert said. "He was worried about losing the food more than safety for himself. He's dedicated."

The side of Rita's mouth quirked upward. "Something about Topazus draws you. Except Katherine of course. I'm glad she finally confessed to the murder, so things won't drag out. She should plead insanity."

"Insanity? Based on what?" Jane asked.

"She holds an irrational dislike for Topazus. After Morgan moved them back here, she finally snapped."

"She didn't have to live in the house," Robert said.

"Another concession poor Morgan had to make. At least he was able to live his last days here and even participated in the pageant one last time."

"What role did he play?" Jane asked.

"The master, of course." She picked up the basket of muffins and passed them.

Rita and Morgan. Lela and Stanford Clark's plan. Was seeing her friend and her husband as mistress and master enough to put Katherine on a path to murder?

Rita sighed. "Now I must prepare for the final

Christmas weekend and the pageant without Micah."

"Is there anything we can do?" Jane asked.

Robert fought the urge to kick Jane's foot under the table.

Rita sent Robert a toothy smile. "I'd be so grateful."

Robert felt the tug of being roped in.

"You and Jane could help by dressing in period costumes on Friday and Saturday. Then be parishioners at the Christmas Eve church service. Micah should be well enough to play his role as a freed slave by then."

She left no pause in her litany to allow declining her invitation.

"Tradition states that the reuniting of the Clark brothers occurred at midnight on Christmas Eve. I play mistress, Cameo the younger sister, James always plays the Union soldier, and a Beau plays the part of the returning Confederate. Cameo and James both complain they are getting too old for the parts. But in the candlelight, who knows? Besides, a genuine descendant always has a part in the pageant and Cameo fulfills that role. Katherine never grasped the value of tradition." She tore off a bite of muffin with a flourish.

"Having a true descendant is a special touch," Jane said.

"Cameo and her grandparents understood. Stanford Clark was wise to protect the Topazus legacy as he did with the trust."

"We'd be glad to help and dress the parts," Jane said.

"We would?" Jane beat him to the foot nudge under the table.

Rita laughed. "I promise it will be painless. You

can dress like you did before."

That was not painless but rather than argue the point Robert would learn what he could from Rita while she was being free with information. "Is there is anything we can do to help you today since Micah is out?"

"This murder has put a chink in your vacation. I hope you don't mind if I take you up on the offer?"

"Not at all." Robert said.

After breakfast Rita directed moving the furniture for activities in the drawing and music rooms. "Part of what we do here at Topazus is to demonstrate how youngsters occupied their time and played in the 1800s. In the drawing room we'll play drop the handkerchief. In the music room, musical chairs."

"Where do you want the love seat?" Robert asked.

"Closer to the fireplace." Rita shook the potpourri on the mantle, helping cover the musty smells around the fireplace. Setting the dish down, she stepped back. "Strange, the mantle clock is missing. Micah must have moved it, but I don't know why he would." Rita shrugged. "I'll ask him when I see him at the hospital later. Are you staying around here today?" she asked.

"We have some investigation assignments this morning, but later Jane and I might steal away to Myrtle Beach and try our luck on the casino ship."

Jane helped Robert position the love seat. "We heard about the ship from the roofer. He goes occasionally and says there's a good buffet and beautiful sunset."

"He saw James there," Robert added. "I thought I'd ask James if he could give me some pointers."

Rita crossed her arms. "Casino boats." She spoke

as though the words tasted bad. "Don't bother. If you want dinner and a lovely sunset, there are plenty of restaurants on the beach."

That touched a sore spot, he'd try another. "We plan to interview merchants in Morgan City this morning and see what they can tell us about Berdanier."

Rita snickered. "Morgan City is short on merchants."

"I still hope to learn more about his habits and clientele. Anything that could point to a possible suspect."

Rita arched her brows. "You don't believe Katherine's confession?"

"Our job is to leave no stone unturned." Robert said.

Rita stared at him a moment, then smiled and wrapped an arm around Jane. "You two do what you think you must. I'll leave a mid-morning snack in the fridge for you because you won't be gone long."

CHAPTER FIFTEEN

In Morgan City, Robert and Jane learned that Berdanier had never been in the Country Cotton Crafts shop, He occasionally purchased a Diet Coke and cinnamon-flavored chewing gum at the Cotton Pickin' Dollar Store. At the Cotton Boll Café, Madison was off, but the waitress on duty said he liked the grilled pork chop special and usually read the newspaper while he ate. No one had an inkling of who might want to see him dead.

A little bell tinkled over the door as they stepped into Cotton Town Jewelers. "This town is hanging by a thread and that thread is cotton," Jane whispered.

A proprietor wearing a headband magnifier came through a curtain from the back. After introductions Robert asked the jeweler, John Oliver, if he had seen or heard anything out of the ordinary pertaining to Berdanier.

"Nope. If you're interested in jewelry, that's what I know about." He glanced toward the room behind the curtain.

"You design your own pieces? These rings are lovely," Jane said, peering into the glass case.

"You bring me a style you like, and I can make it."

"Did you make the replica of the Topazus ring?" Jane asked.

"I ..." Oliver's eyes narrowed. "Berdanier ... he wanted it made."

"I saw the real one years ago." Jane shot him a fetching smile. "The copy you made is a remarkable likeness."

The jeweler softened. "You can't get the same topaz brightness with quartz." He unlocked the display case with a key clipped to a lanyard hanging around his neck. He slid the cabinet door open and took out a ring. "This is a quartz made in a similar style."

Jane held the ring, twisting it to catch the light. "Simply enchanting."

"Did Mr. Berdanier discuss the Topazus ring theft?" Robert asked.

The smile slid from Oliver's face.

"All he said was he wanted one made like it and handed me a picture."

The magic gone. He shoved the ring Jane returned to him back in its holder and closed the display door with a *thunk*. "I'm busy in the back." He re-locked the case. "Anything else?" He parted the curtain. A man in a gray suit stood behind the curtain, his back to them.

"No sir. Thanks for the information." They departed to the sound of the tinkling bell.

"Testy body language." Jane said.

"Hmm. He was agitated at the mention of Berdanier."

"I thought he was annoyed because we weren't there to buy anything," Jane said.

"That too I suspect." A tent sign for King Cotton Antiques of the South stood in front of them on the sidewalk. "Let's see if there's anything more we can learn from Ms. Hangstrom."

Inside, Ms. Hangstrom was on the phone in the back and waved at them. The store window held the pine-scented nostalgic display of a Christmas tree decorated with construction paper chains and old-fashioned bubble lights.

"My grandma's tree had lights like that." Jane pointed to the teddy bear sitting in a child's rocker beside the tree. "I used to watch the bubbles and rock my Baby Sparkles."

"The baby sparkled?"

"She did. Her crown, earrings and heart lit up."

The glint in Jane's eyes lit Robert's spirit. "Good memories are nice to hold onto."

"Hi folks." Ms. Hangstrom joined them. "How is your investigation progressing?"

"Still fact-gathering," Robert said. "Merchants we talked to say Mr. Berdanier kept to himself, so we haven't learned very much."

"You would think Morgan City would be small enough to know what was going on, but what you are hearing is right. He did keep to himself. Always came and went from the back."

Ms. Hangstrom tapped her cheek. "Remember me telling you about the Topazus clock? The man who brought it in just left Berdanier's office."

"Oh?"

"He was with a lady. Cameo Clark." She grinned.

"I popped over to speak to them."

Mrs. Hangstrom was an investigator's dream. Nosy and talkative. "She's the attorney we're working for. She was with the man who brought the clock in?"

"Yes, at least I think it was him. He didn't seem to recognize me and was preoccupied with some paperwork. They left a few minutes ago." She stepped to the glass rear door of the shop and peered out. "Looks like they may have dropped a paper."

Robert walked to the rear door. "I'll retrieve the paper and throw it away if it isn't important. If anything turns up," Robert handed her his card, "I'd appreciate a call."

Outside, Robert picked up the paper that Ms. Hangstrom spotted and whistled through his teeth.

"What is it?" Jane asked.

"A memo from James to Cameo dated a month ago. He scanned the message while Jane looked on.

"Am I reading this right? James heard about the mineral lease Berdanier was negotiating with Roger Underwood and informed Cameo?" Jane asked.

"Looks like it."

"Cameo said she was in the dark, but if she knew about the negotiations—"

Robert's phone buzzed, and he checked the screen. "Vance Freed." He motioned for Jane to write.

"Hello Vance, any news for me?" He opened the passenger door of his truck for Jane.

"I had to use more of my blue chips getting this done pronto for you." Vance said.

"That makes three steak dinners I owe you?"

"Four. But who's counting?"

"You apparently. I'm putting you on speaker so

Jane can get this down."

"Howdy Jane."

Robert held the phone up for her. "Howdy back."

"What have you got for me?" Robert asked.

"It's pretty simple. Ashes from the primary sample taken by the grill were found on the shoes and cart one," Vance said.

"Both pairs of shoes?"

"Right, the dress and garden shoes. Now the Styrofoam cups examined by our fingerprint man didn't yield very good prints, but he matched a partial on a thumbprint to the one on the drive. It belongs to Cameo Clark."

~

Leaving Morgan City, Jane rolled down the passenger window. The buzzing of the truck's tires against the pavement provided background noise to her unsettled thoughts.

"It's not surprising Cameo's thumb print was on the drive since she placed it in the port, right?" Jane asked.

"Yes, but what if she took advantage of the lights going out and hid it?" Robert said.

"But why?" Jane's voice cracked.

Robert held up his index finger. "Theory. She leaves us in the library to get her laptop and has second thoughts about what might be revealed on the drive. When the lights go out, she seizes the opportunity to take the drive, hides it and doesn't have to make explanations."

"Yes, but it was still hidden two days later."

"Cameo said she no longer needed the drive when

she was allowed access to Berdanier's computer."

Robert's theory didn't make sense. Cameo seemed genuinely interested in seeing the drive before the lights went out. "Want my theory?"

"Shoot."

"The lights were shut off on purpose. In the confusion, the perpetrator entered the room. Sneezed. Stepped on my foot and pulled the drive out by the sides thereby not smudging Cameo's print. This someone was knowledgeable about secret places in the house and hid it."

"And the reason?" Robert asked.

"To see what was on it."

"So why was it still there Monday?"

"Um … we already came up with the theory that the thief couldn't find the right time to retrieve it without being seen. Surely you don't think your theory is more plausible than mine."

He shrugged and went silent.

They passed leafless trees with sinewy branches pointing in all directions, like a traffic cop who couldn't decide which way to direct cars. Jane picked up the memo that had been dropped. "Cameo said she was in the dark about mineral leasing but if she knew... and Berdanier counters by bringing up the vehicular homicide victim …"

"It gives Cameo a strong motive to be rid of Berdanier and end the trust," Robert said.

Could Cameo be the killer? The idea made Jane queasy. She gave Robert a sideward glance. He caught her eye and patted her knee. "Hey, this is sheer speculation and the computer drive may be of little consequence."

"So now what do we do?"
"Return to the scene of the crime."

CHAPTER SIXTEEN

Robert wheeled into the Topazus entrance and punched in the key code. The black iron gate swung open—an invitation to a mystery yet to be solved. Was he up to the challenge?

Could he read the clues as he used? Or was the only reason for his success in solving crimes in the past due to the resources that had been available to him from the State of Alabama?

Currently he was forced to rely on favors from his ABI buddy for help with evidence. But at least he had that, and he'd have to work with it. He drove through the gate, pulled off the side of the drive and turned off the ignition. "With the latest evidence, I believe following the trail of ashes is going to be the key to the killer."

Robert slid from his seat and circled the truck to open Jane's door, but she had gotten out already, purse hung on her shoulder.

"The trail of ashes. It sounds like a book title."

Working with a schoolteacher cast a unique twist on the investigation. "There may be one by that title in the Topazus library." He smiled at her. "Come on."

With Jane at his side, they walked the trail of packed dirt covered by pine needles that disappeared into the woods.

"We're looking for ashes on the trail?"

"No. I want to examine the area where the forensics report indicated the shot came from. Then I believe the trail of ashes will materialize."

"How do they establish where a shot originates?"

"Math and physics. I always relied on what the experts determined when working a shooting. In this case, we have the information given to us in discovery from those who worked the crime scene."

The path brought them to a tree-covered alcove a few degrees cooler than the sunny sixties they'd stepped out of.

"It's secluded and lovely here, there's even a bench." Jane walked over and sat down.

Robert did a 360 and scrutinized the area. "The diagram in the report shows this trail leads to a Y at the bottom of the hill. Left leads to the mansion and right travels up the hill to Crest Manor."

He stepped to a spot beside a pine tree where there was an unobstructed view to the gate. Robert held his arm straight out and sighted down his imaginary rifle. "The crime scene analysis showed the shooter stood here. There is a straight shot to the spot where Berdanier would have stopped his car waiting for the gate to open." He dropped his arm. The underbrush of pinecones and thorny greenbrier vines snagged at his ankles.

Robert turned around. "The killer might have sat where you are, waiting to shoot Berdanier."

"That gives me the shivers," Jane said.

Robert sat beside her. The cold wrought-iron seat sapped the heat from his legs. "This seat is frigid. No wonder you have the shivers. Let's ponder the ashes."

"Ashes. That will warm things up."

Amazing. Finding a positive spin was second nature to her. Jane dug her notepad from her purse. He generally operated from the movie camera in his head, visualizing scenarios, but she liked to put pen to paper.

"Cart one had traces of the grill ashes. If the murderer got ashes on his or her shoes when they accessed the gun and the ashes later turned up on my shoes, the greatest likelihood is that the transfer took place in the cart."

"So maybe ID who we know drove the carts and when?" Jane drew two squares on her paper and labeled them cart #1 and #2.

"We rode in the cart which would have been number two, to the murder scene and Cameo drove."

"That's the one without the reindeer ornament." Jane made a notation.

"The cart Rita and Micah arrived in; I drove back to the mansion. Did you see who drove that cart when they arrived?"

Jane pressed her lips together. "Um … no. I was watching you talk to the officer about roping off the crime scene. They were already outside the cart when I noticed them."

"Okay, so Micah or Rita drove the cart that has the number one mini-plate."

Jane drew a reindeer head next to cart number one

on her paper.

"Cart one is the likely place I picked up the ashes. Let's consider who could have driven the cart after the luncheon." Cameo concerned him. The motive to be rid of Berdanier was strong, but what about her opportunity considering the latest evidence. Was the reason she didn't believe her mother shot Berdanier because she shot him?

"Take Cameo first," Robert said. "Cameo could have driven cart one to Crest Manor while we waited on her in library. She walks through the ashes, gets her mother's gun, drives the cart to the gate, shoots Berdanier, returns the gun and drives back in cart one, leaving ashes on the pedals."

"Then ashes, in turn, get on your shoes when you drive the cart back to the mansion after the interviews at the murder scene." Jane scribbled notes, then tossed her pen on the pad. "I don't buy it. We've hashed over all that before."

"Except now we have stronger motive. You have to sift through clues and continue to examine them from different angles."

"Okay. Explain the connection between Cameo and the garden shoes."

Robert slapped his thigh. "That shifts some suspicion off Cameo."

"We said earlier that it doesn't seem likely Cameo went in kitchen and put on those shoes unnoticed." Jane lifted her shoulders and let them drop. "To me, those who went in the kitchen after the luncheon might be more suspect."

He appreciated Jane's analytics. Robert closed his eyes visualizing the dining room after lunch. "That would be Micah, Mary Sue and then Rita."

"Is there any other explanation for the grill ashes being on the garden shoes?" Jane asked.

"Maybe picking up residue from the cart pedals as I did?" Robert stood and paced in front of the bench. Movement helped him think. "The ashes were noticeable on the top of the garden shoes when I was talking to you after the mother-daughter tea. That was the morning after the murder. From analysis, we know there was residue from the grill on the bottom of those shoes so powder on top of the shoes could indicate walking *through* ashes to retrieve the gun."

"If the ashes on the garden shoes point to the killer then you feel that Rita, Micah or Mary Sue are the best candidates?" Jane circled the names as she read them off and then drew a giant question mark. "What drives someone to murder?"

Robert returned to his seat, leaned back against the hard bench, and crossed his legs at the ankles. He'd discussed that question many times with his cohorts and had come to a simple conclusion. "Passion on steroids. That's my short answer. At a crime scene seminar, the presenter boiled the reasons into four Ls. Love, lust, loot, and loathing. Those four create an umbrella where you can categorize the root of all murder motives according to him. I've found his notion to be fairly accurate."

Jane steepled her hands under her chin. "It's a paradox for love to make the list, but they say love hurts." Jane said.

"Exactly. Love opens you to vulnerability and that means you can hurt and be hurt whether intentional or not."

"Like me and my brother?"

"To a degree. You had pinned your hurt on Adam and never gave a thought to what he might be experiencing. Hurt became magnified because you cared. It's when people let that caring passion become exaggerated and out of control that the urge to kill can overtake. In the case of Berdanier's demise, I don't think we're looking at love or lust."

"You think loathing or loot?"

"I'd say so. Loathing could include anger and maybe fear of exposure. Katherine and Cameo exhibited both those possibilities with the vehicular homicide hanging over Cameo."

"What about loot?"

"Inheritance and subsidiary gain to that inheritance. Those reasons are all wrapped up in Cameo becoming owner of the property." Robert envisioned Rita and James buddying up with Cameo.

"And whoever attaches to Cameo will benefit with Berdanier out of the way. James seems to be attaching to Cameo," Jane said.

Robert scooted to an upright position and glanced at Jane. Amazing. Jane's thoughts matched his. "Yes. Another subsidiary to gain with James and Cameo connecting would be Rita. Loot for her is tied to her catering business, which she'd lose if the property is sold. Bigger than that is the insurance payoff. Since the insurance from the theft of the ring is already invested in the property, if the theft was a hoax, exposure might be reason to kill."

"Which L is exposure?"

"Two Ls—loathing exposure of $50,000 in fraudulent loot gain."

Jane crossed her arms and sighed. "It is not unusual for people to experience lust, love and loathing and even to seek loot, but the vast majority don't murder."

Robert took in the shaded wintry landscape. "Therein lies the dark side of human nature. I think it's related to what the preacher talked about Sunday."

"You mean about people wearing masks?"

"Yes. Which, as you say, is not that unusual. But some go deeper and darker and are pressed to do unseemly deeds while under the protection and cover of their mask. Secrecy is what ignites and gives power to the seamier sides of the four Ls."

"So, what's the answer? How do you stop people from going too deep?"

"An age-old question. That goes back to Cain killing Abel."

"Jealousy on steroids?"

She did it again. "You unmask my thinking as we talk."

"Hey." She jerked her head and stared at him. "That's it. We're talking. The preacher said the remedy for hiding behind our masks is talking and conversing with God. We do that in prayer, but it's also important to take off masks and talk to each other."

Her openness was refreshing. "Nothing hard about the remedy. Applying it is difficult."

"That's true with my brother." Jane stood. A spark in her eye. "I was so disillusioned and upset at the loss of our close relationship, but once he told me about his kidney problem— took off his mask—we've been able to talk again. Hiding his problem, he thought, was the loving thing to do. But it's a prime example of the brooding and hurt that being secretive can bring."

Jane's being able to heal the wound she carried regarding her brother warmed his soul. "Now that we've discovered the root and cure to man's grim side, do you think we can apply it to our problem at hand?"

Jane's eyes went wide. "I'm babbling and we have a murder to solve." She sat down, a pushed her hair back from her face. "Let's see ...," she tapped her finger to her lips, "... application."

He could feel heat radiating from her.

"I've got it. Topazus wears a mask."

"O ... kay." Not expected. "Like ... the place is lovely on the outside and moldy and rat infested on the inside?" Robert tried to tune into her point.

"See? Topazus needs to risk exposure and tell us what she needs."

Robert laughed. "I'll stick to talking to people."

"Stay with me. I'm talking personification ... the house is weeping—"

"That sounds more like English lit than keys to killing—"

Jane jumped off the bench. She grabbed something from the ground. Was she going to hit him? She shoved a pinecone under his nose.

"There's. Our. Proof." Her words came out one at a time and reached a crescendo. "See?"

"Uh... I can't see with my nose." Jane shifted the pinecone with its prickly points directly in front of his eyes.

"Look at the bottom. It's trimmed." The pinecone was altered like the one Katherine showed Jane how to trim.

"This cone is like the ones that spilled from the box

on the cart you drove. The shooter was here and so was cart number one."

~

Jane set the pinecone discovery on the desk in her room and flopped on the bed. What a day. Robert had agreed the pinecone find was important. Added to the other clues, where would it lead?

He'd apologized that the Christmas retreat had deteriorated into work. "Get some rest while you can before Cameo gets back."

She closed her eyes. No deal. Her eyes popped open, and her feet hit the floor. Too wired. Something niggled. What? She stepped to the desk, picked up the trimmed pinecone and touched the tip that would become a reindeer's nose. A cone without its reindeer mask. Was she missing the obvious? Who prepared the cones? Katherine. Did she have prepared cones on cart number three kept at Crest Manor? Did one fall off at the shooter site? Ashes weren't found on her cart, but she said she changed her shoes. Were the police right? Was her confession genuine?

Her phone buzzed. Robert.

"Sorry. No time for rest. Cameo is back."

~

When Jane entered the Topazus kitchen with Robert, Cameo, James and Rita were deep in conversation.

Cameo, mid-sentence, lifted her hand in welcome and pointed Jane and Robert to empty chairs at the Topazus kitchen table. "As much as I tried to dissuade her, mother is still adamant that she shot Berdanier. She says she'll plead guilty at the preliminary hearing and put everyone out of their misery."

Robert had put Jane under his rule number nine "gag order," wanting her to take in more information than she gave out. He need not worry. She wasn't eager to share the pinecone discovery that might bolster Katherine's admission of guilt.

"Are you sure we should go on with the weekend events with all this hanging over you, dear?" Rita patted Cameo's wrist with one hand and slid a tray of crackers, meats, and cheeses toward Jane and Robert with the other.

"I asked mother and she is resigned to the activities proceeding. She is not involved this weekend's activities anyhow."

Rita blew out a burst of tense air and sniffed. "Well ... if you're sure." With neither her Christmas events nor her conversation being disrupted, she deftly poured coffee into two mugs, handed them to Jane and Robert and pointed to cream and sugar. "I'm glad you two are here because I have plans mapped out," she hesitated and looked at Cameo, "pending your okay, of course."

Cameo returned a weak smile.

"Tomorrow night, gates open at 5:30. As with all the Friday events, there will be the bonfire and caroling. Micah is out of the hospital but must take it easy. His son, Casey, will handle the bonfire. Belles and Beaus will be in charge of the lantern light garden tours and the Christmas caroling."

She rattled off plans like a train gathering speed, but Jane slipped in a question. "Do the Belles and Beaus sing?"

"They might sing along, but volunteers from area churches do the caroling. I've trained the Belles and Beaus to greet and direct the carolers to meander about the gardens and bonfire." Rita held her shoulders back and the kitchen light caught the gleam in her eyes. "The grounds come alive with song as the guests join in singing Christmas favorites. It's wonderful." She rested her hand at the base of her throat, seeming to be enthralled by her own vision. "I will play Martha Lee's role as the mother who has gone through the ravages of the Civil War in which her sons fought on opposing sides."

"You don't present the history of the house?" Robert asked.

"Not on the weekend before Christmas. This presentation is one that Cameo's grandmother developed as a prelude to the Topazus Christmas Eve service. I give a special invitation for people to return for the candlelight ceremony depicting the reuniting of the Clark brothers. This year marks 154 years since their return."

"It's important to keep the tradition alive," Cameo said. "But do James and I have to continue playing the brother and sister parts?"

"Yeah." James presented a pained expression. "I'm a good fifteen years older than Daniel is supposed to be."

Rita looked at Jane and Robert. "I told you they would complain." With a wave of her hand, she dismissed their objection and continued her discourse.

"After I present the history there will be games in the music room and drawing room. In the library, Jane and Robert, I thought you might take turns reading about the tradition of the Yule log and Christmas sweets."

Rita held up the carafe, making eye contact with

each of those in her audience. James took her offer, holding out his cup. Rita poured but maintained the dialogue. "There is a Yule log that burns in the bonfire and there will be a Yule log cake for refreshments in the dining room." Tapping the table in front of Cameo, she said, "As always, you play Sarah, and James, you're Daniel, in the music room. Mary Sue will handle refreshments."

James sighed and looked heavenward. "Like I say, at thirty-nine I'm a bit old to be playing a soldier of twenty-three."

Rita clapped her hands as Jane had often done to settle her kindergarten class. "If you stay in character, no one will care."

Turning her focus on Robert and Jane again, Rita said, "You two were perfect last week as my cousin Camilla and her husband from Boston. Are you okay with that?"

Robert straightened in his seat. "I'm okay with it if I have a name like everyone else."

"Oh?" Rita seemed stunned at the interruption. She stared at Robert.

Jane struggled to keep a straight face. What was Robert up to?

A smile gradually overtook Rita's face. "Well, of course. You should have a name. What name would you like? It would need to be in keeping with the 1800s, you understand. Horatio maybe?"

Robert shook his head, "Too educated sounding."

"Reginald?"

"Too sophisticated."

Jane giggled.

Rita frowned. "What do you have in mind?"

"How about George?"

Cameo laughed. "Why George?"

"The name sounds ... regal. You know, like King George."

"And since you're from Boston," James said, "what about Austin for a last name? You will be Camilla and George Austin from Boston. Like your Aunt Bessie Lawrence from Florence," James said to Jane.

It was Jane's turn to be stunned. When Jane made that comment, she and Robert were alone in the library. "How did you know about my Aunt Bessie?"

"Oh," James cut his eyes to Cameo, "Cameo told me I think." Was he hoping she'd save him?

Cameo shrugged. "First I've heard of Aunt Bessie Lawrence from Florence. Cute though. I like the Austins from Boston." She patted James on the shoulder.

With a roll of her eyes and a tilt of her head toward the door, Jane gave Robert what she hoped was an I-need-to-talk-to-you look.

Rita finished with instructions about how they were to dress and Robert said, "If you don't need us for anything else right now, Jane and I would like to be excused to write up reports from our interviews today."

Outside, Jane whispered, "Let's talk in my room." Clues coming to light had ramped up her pulse rate. She unlocked the door to her room and snapped on the desk light.

Robert closed the door behind them and cocked his head. "You're concerned about the Aunt Bessie comment?"

"Yes. We were by ourselves when I mentioned

Lawrence rhyming with Florence." Jane sat on the desk chair, leaned forward, and rested her arms on her knees. "You and I sat down to fix tea. Cameo had gone to get her laptop and phone she'd left in her charger."

Robert stroked his heavy stubbled chin. "You talked about seeing the original ring when you came with your aunt."

"Right. I talked about how brilliant the stone was, and we speculated about the computer drive ... and what information might be on it about the ring."

Robert plunked down in the side chair. "The lights went out and James showed up with a flashlight."

"See? He had to have been listening." Jane pressed her hands against her knees. "Possibly from the hidden space between the walls."

"And he felt the need to hide the drive."

Stray bits of information whirled in her head: the missing drive, the pinecone, vehicular homicide, ashes, her aunt from Florence. Jane's neck muscles developed a pesky tic.

Shouldn't the scattered clues somehow fit together to form a picture of who shot Berdanier? Or were they just indicators? Like the wintry tree branches pointing every which way? Jane's inner teacher preferred things to be neat, desks aligned, students forming straight lines.

"What does it all mean? Can you make sense of the information we've gathered?"

Robert stood; his eyes, intense, held hers. "I don't know. But I have an idea of how to find out."

CHAPTER SEVENTEEN

SLED Officer Kelley had agreed to meet at the Bennett County Sheriff's Office annex between Morgan City and Granite Ridge.

Robert and Jane's footsteps clanged on the aluminum steps of the portable office. Inside, Officer Kelley greeted them and pointed to guest chairs in front of the desk with Deputy Norwood's nameplate.

Robert adjusted his collar. The office was warm, stuffy, and held the strong odor of coffee cooked to syrup stage.

"I'd offer you coffee but I'm thinking it is beyond drinkable, even for a lawman," Kelley said.

"I won't challenge that statement." Robert offered a firm handshake "That stuff smells like it might qualify for drain cleaner. Thanks for meeting us on short notice."

"No problem. I was in the vicinity. Norwood had to answer a call, so we have the place to ourselves."

Officer Kelley sat behind the desk; the position Robert had occupied most of his twenty-five law enforcement years. Now he was in the position of meddler, the kind that officers wished would mind their own business.

Kelley leaned back in the chair. "So ... what did you want to discuss?" His eyes said to get on with whatever he had to say because he had better ways to spend his time.

"I've read the information provided after Katherine Clark's arrest and we are doing follow-up investigation for the defense."

"I understand." Kelley tapped his steepled hands together.

The agent's body language told Robert his time was limited. No time for chit-chat. So, he jumped right in with his supposition. "Ashes under the grill and next to the .22 rifle, which has been identified as the murder weapon, have turned up in other places."

Kelley hiked a brow. "What places?"

"The garden shoes in Rita Parsons' office, Topazus cart one and on my shoes."

Officer Kelley snickered. "Should I add you to the suspect list?"

Had Robert ever been guilty of showing the snide attitude Kelley presented? Probably. He continued. "Since the fact that Katherine's .22 was next to the grill has been corroborated, anyone who took the gun would have had to walk through those ashes to get to the rifle. If the ashes turned up in other places, there are conceivably other suspects."

"Based on tracked ashes? Maybe someone stepped where Katherine Clark walked and tracked ashes from there."

"Not in the quantity we found. Topazus has three numbered electric carts used to move around the estate. Carts one and two stay behind the Topazus kitchen, cart three stays at Crest Manor.

"When I drove cart one from the murder scene, ashes now identified as coming from the grill, got on my shoes. Later I noticed ashes on the clogs kept beside the kitchen utility porch. When I realized the ashes might be meaningful, I gathered samples from the shoes and carts and had them analyzed. Lab results confirmed that ashes from the grill matched those on my shoes, the garden shoes, and cart one."

Officer Kelley crossed his arms and frowned. "And what is your conclusion from this fascinating information?"

"That the person who wore those garden shoes and drove cart one was at Crest Manor and walked in the grill ashes where they could have accessed the gun." Robert pointed to himself. "I know I didn't walk in the ashes at Crest Manor, but they got on my shoes. There were no grill ashes in the Crest Manor cart and should have been if Katherine retrieved the gun."

"That grill had been turned over the night before. Katherine could have driven cart one at some point."

"That's far-fetched. Why walk down that steep hill and around the mansion to the kitchen to drive a cart when there is a cart that stays at Crest Manor?"

"Look." Officer Kelley stood. "You don't think it's far-fetched to say someone put on garden shoes ran up to Crest Manor tromped through the ashes, grabbed the rifle, shot Berdanier and then returned the gun?" His tone was steamy and his patience dwindling.

"Yes. But if you add driving a cart there and back, it changes from far-fetched to possible. Rita drove to the murder site with Micah in cart one. Micah had to leave and asked me to drive cart one while Cameo and Rita drove cart two back to the main house."

"Were Rita or Micah wearing garden shoes when they arrived at the murder scene?" Kelley asked.

"Slipping on the garden clogs would have been temporary," Robert said.

Jane had her notepad out and raised her pen to speak. "At the murder scene, Rita had on the low-heeled shoes she wore to the luncheon. I noticed because she had mentioned they hurt her feet."

Officer Kelley blew out a puff of air and held up his hands. "This is all very interesting, but is that it?"

"No. There's a matter of a missing computer jump drive from Berdanier's office that went missing and—"

Kelley's brows shot up. "Wait. You took a jump drive from Berdanier's workplace? You of all people know not to tamper with things that could be of evidentiary value."

The SLED officer's abrasive attitude was wearing on Robert. "We had a key. You had no search warrant."

Kelley's roughed up feathers remained stirred, but he knew that technically Robert was right. "What was on it?" he grumbled.

"Issues mentioned during the dicey conversation at the luncheon before Berdanier was shot. Little content. Basically, a topic list related to the trust and Topazus. Since you had Berdanier's hard files and computer, you had access to more complete information."

Robert repositioned on the edge of his chair. "What's noteworthy is the drive was stolen before we had a chance to see all that was on it. It was hidden in a secret drawer in the library at the mansion, and Jane and I happened to find it. We suspect someone needed to buy time before certain issues came to light. Remember the unlatched briefcase at the murder scene?"

"Okay." Kelley removed his glasses and pinched the bridge of his nose and then resettled them. "Someone was curious about a drive that held little information. So what?"

"Someone feared what *might* have been on it. You have to admit the ashes and hiding the drive add evidence that needs to be accounted for."

Kelley stood. "First of all, I don't *have* to admit anything. This doesn't change the fact that Katherine Clark threatened Berdanier, and her gun fired the shot that killed the man."

"Hear me out." Robert's window of opportunity to get through to Agent Kelley was closing fast. "On Berdanier's list of things to discuss was the Topazus ring. We believe the ring was fraudulently reported stolen by Rita Parsons for the insurance money. What if Berdanier knew and was going to blow the whistle on the false report? Insurance paid fifty thousand dollars. People have killed for less."

"Are you suggesting Rita Parsons—"

Here was his chance. "I'm suggesting setting up a situation to bring the Topazus ring out of hiding."

"Ashes, missing drives and a stolen ring that was not stolen." Kelley shook his head and stood. "I'm sorry but aren't you grasping at straws? And flimsy straws at that. You're trying to cast doubt on a good arrest. I heard through the grapevine that Mrs. Clark has now confessed."

"I believe she is covering for someone."

Kelley dropped his head, huffed and sat on the edge of the desk. "Listen. It's been a long day for me. I understand your job is to pull out the stops for your client. But you haven't been away from working as a lawman long enough to have forgotten that we have an excellent case." He peered over his glasses. "I've looked into your background."

The agent's demeanor and words felt like a weight being pressed hard against his chest. Tarnish on a good name is hard to wipe clean.

"You no longer have arrest power and you need someone who does to help with your theory. But I'm not real sure what that theory is. I think we're wasting each other's time."

Agent Kelley was letting Robert know, in a not-so-subtle way, that he regarded Robert as a washed-up cop who was working on the wrong side of justice, trying to get a criminal off the hook. In Kelley's eyes, Robert fit the description of traitor, casting doubt on law enforcement's work.

Robert stood motioning to Jane. "Yes. We have taken enough of your time. We'll get out of your hair." He started to follow Jane to the door but tossed one more item to Agent Kelley. "A tip. Keep an eye on the jeweler, John Oliver, in Morgan City."

Outside, Jane began rummaging in her purse. "I left my pen in there. I'll be right back."

"I've got a pen. Leave it."

"No. I'm partial to my pen."

She was gone for only a minute, but long enough for Robert to stew over his own feelings of being on the wrong side of the law.

CHAPTER EIGHTEEN

Beaus and Belles had transformed into characters of the 1800s and were outside preparing for the lantern tour in the garden.

Inside the Topazus dressing room, the pungent odor of the oil burning lamp on the dresser overpowered the perfumed potpourri. Robert submitted to Jane's inspection. "Stand straight and let me fix your collar." The flickering lamp light cast distorted shadows across her face and the other house tour participants.

"These crinolines are noisy and this corset pinches," Cameo complained.

"But you look the part of a twenty-year-old little sister." James fiddled with the cuff links at his wrists.

"You are a charmer, brother Daniel, but I'll thank the dim lantern light."

"You both look your parts. Burnt orange is your color Cameo," Jane said.

"Why I declare, Cousin Camilla, you are all kindness. If George wasn't yours, I'd swoon." Cameo feigned fanning herself with her hand.

For an instant, Jane's response and possessive clasp on his arm made Robert forget the evening's grave mission. "You mustn't be greedy, Sarah."

"You have your instructions," Rita cut in, "remember them." Dressed in a gown of deep blue, she placed the Topazus ring copy on her gloved finger. "Guests will arrive soon. Sarah and Daniel go downstairs. I have the CD player hidden behind the curtain in the music room. Start the music and keep it low."

Rita had a plan and so did Robert. Exactly how it would unfold could not be scripted. His strategy was a risk. However, if the gut feeling he had trusted for years in law enforcement was still operational, his vibes meant he was on the right track. Tonight's scheme could prove his suspicions. Or if it backfired, could bring his ability as a detective into question. And worse, if he failed, hurt his client.

James ushered Cameo out of the dressing room into the hall, her skirts rustling.

Robert set his gaze on Rita. With her posture straight, chin lifted, eyes glassy, she gazed in the dresser mirror and adjusted the tiara in her blond, gray-streaked hair. The frame of the mirror became the picture frame of the portrait downstairs of Martha Lee Clark. Rita had become the mistress of Topazus.

She turned from the mirror and addressed Jane and Robert; the only ones left in the room. Her voice was a shade deeper and the tone more authoritative. "After I recite the story of my twin boys who fought on opposite sides of the war, I will send part of our guests to the music room and part to the library. The groups will switch and then be escorted to the dining room. Once there, I'll bring in a new group."

"Everything is well planned, Martha Lee." Robert said.

She returned a half-shrug. "I've been mistress long enough. The evening should run smoothly."

With Jane at his side, Robert said, "Shouldn't you be wearing the real Topazus ring? Camilla says the ring you're wearing is a copy and isn't as vibrant as the real thing."

Rita fixed penetrating eyes on him, then shifted to Jane. Her brows creased together. Had he messed up and shown his hand too quickly? If he had, there was no way he'd be able to recreate the opportunity without garnering suspicion. He remained still and expectant.

"Daniel says I should keep it tucked away for safety," Rita said.

Jane gripped Robert's arm so hard bruising was inevitable. But when she spoke, her words sounded natural and pleasant. "What good is it to have the real thing, cousin, if you have to wear a copy?"

"A shame." Robert lifted his shoulders. "What would it hurt if you took it out just long enough to show it to us?"

Rita gave a furtive glance at the door. Strains of instrumental music reached them. "I suppose it wouldn't hurt. Our secret?"

Robert's insides vibrated. Rita stepped to the dresser. She opened the jewelry box, took out the pin cushion and tilted the box sideways. There was a swishing sound and a soft *clunk*. A drawer sliding open? A strangled cry came out of her throat.

James appeared in the doorway. "Where's the

Sousa march—" His eyes went to the jewelry box, slid to his mother and then traveled to Robert and Jane. "What … are you doing?" His voice slow and even, as if walking on partially frozen ice.

"Daniel. The ring. Where is it?" Rita's voice a piteous whine.

"The ring was stolen. It's gone. Remember?"

Rita frowned and held up the empty drawer. Confusion in her eyes. "We keep it in here."

"Mother, you're confused." James took a step toward Rita.

Her jaw tightened and speech quickened. "Confused?... No ... no ... we got rid of him, so we wouldn't have to worry. Where is the ring?" The word 'ring' caught in her throat. "You said …" Rita's face contorted. "You told me it would be all right to wear the ring for special events." She moaned and tears spilled onto her cheeks.

James took another cautious step. He held up the palm of his hand as if approaching a cornered animal. "You don't know what you're saying. Listen to me. You are not Martha Lee. The guests aren't here yet."

She stared at him a long moment. She clenched the empty drawer she'd taken from inside the jewelry box. "You took it." Her voice low, menacing. "Didn't you?" Her eyes glistened in the lamplight with the dark intensity of deep, black water. "Where is it? You're the only one who knows about the drawer inside the jewelry box." Her face twisted into a sour, tortured expression. Her eyes sent daggers.

"Mother," He inched closer. "It's me, James. You are not Martha Lee. The ring was stolen."

"I know who I am! And I know exactly who you

are. You're a fool!" She spat the words in tight, accusing jabs. "A fool who gambles and gets into debt. And then tries to get out of debt by gambling some more." She took a step toward him. Her face flushed. "Money has disappeared from the savings account. Then expensive items at home ... the Dresden mantle clock. We removed Berdanier. The ring was safe. And now ... How could you?" Her words struck like the bite of a venomous snake.

James reached out to touch her shoulder.

Rita reared her arm back. "Fool!" The smack to his face sounded at the same time her elbow hit the lamp on the dresser, slamming it against the wall and soaking the curtains in lamp oil. Fire streaked up the curtains to the ceiling like a flash of lightning. James grabbed his mother, who struggled against his grasp. "Don't touch me."

Robert snatched the closet door open and Officer Kelley stepped out. He nodded and held up a microcassette recorder.

Smoke filled the room. Everyone moved toward the door. James took his mother by the shoulders and pushed her through the doorway. She continued to slap at him; her face red and tear streaked.

Cameo's voice yelled from downstairs. "Fire! Get out now!"

Smoke rose up the stairwell. Robert turned and grabbed Jane's arm. Putting her in front of him, he steered her out of the room. Across the hall, flames licked at the ceiling and the wall next to the fireplace. Jane yelped. Robert felt something wallop his leg. Two huge rats with tails like whips sailed across his feet and scampered down the stairs ahead of them.

Reaching the main hall, James helped Cameo but had to shove his mother out the back door.

Mary Sue rushed from the dining room. "Oh, my God. Fire is spreading everywhere. I tried to use the kitchen fire extinguisher, but there's no stopping it."

Robert and Officer Kelley helped guide Mary Sue and Jane in their cumbersome hooped skirts out the rear door. Smoke burned Robert's eyes as the roar of fire deepened and heat bore down on his backside.

Outside Cameo was on her phone. Perspiration matted her hair to her forehead. She walked backward on the garden path, watching Topazus burn while reporting the fire. Micah's boy, Casey, struggled with the garden hose beside the bonfire and tried to angle it toward the mansion. The spray did nothing to slow the hungry flames gulping the window frames.

Robert shielded Jane, the intense heat driving all the spectators further down the garden path, away from the conflagration.

James attempted to console his mother. She shrieked, "Leave me alone! This is your fault!" She jerked from him and stood staring at Topazus, the light from the flames flickering in her eyes. Cameo touched her shoulder. "Rita, we need to move back."

Belles and Beaus moved toward the pavilion beside the bed-and-breakfast unit for shelter.

Sirens could be heard in the distance. Cameo called her mother at Crest Manor to open the gates for the fire trucks.

Rita sobbed while Cameo, her arm wrapped about her shoulder, encouraged her to sit on a bench seat opposite Jane and Robert. James shrunk away from the others, wringing his hands. Agent Kelley stood behind them.

Robert had received Agent Kelley's call that afternoon, saying he'd had second thoughts. He agreed to try out Robert's theory. The cost to Agent Kelley was a little more of his time. But the risk to Robert if his plan failed, was an additional loss of reputation in law enforcement circles.

If he could coax Rita to bring the ring out of hiding, it would prove fraud. Fear of blackmail presented a compelling motive for murder. But more than that, he believed the man who said, "Don't worry you'll get your money," the man who knew the Aunt Bessie rhyme, the man in the gray suit behind the jeweler's curtain—the renaissance man—was also the man involved in Berdanier's murder.

Scorching heat fumed. Raging flames engulfed the house. Fire reached, twisted, and twirled in frenzied abandon. Topazus showing off. Her mask removed. She laughed at the paltry bonfire. The mansion, bursting from confinement, exposed and cleansed its long-held secrets. Exploding in a blazing display of its own. Tonight, the house rivaled the brilliance of the celebrated Topazus ring.

The siren grew louder, the flash of red lights pierced the trees of the forested drive with the arrival of the fire truck. Men poured out, grabbing gear and hoisting hoses. In seconds, they battled the flames with a heavy force of water, then saturated the surroundings to prevent the fire from spreading.

"Like kindling wood," Robert said.

"What's that?" Officer Kelley asked.

"Kindling. Alfred Berdanier had said insurance was too costly. The aging house was so old, that if there was a fire, the dried pine would flare up like kindling wood."

"Fifty years." Rita whimpered; her eyes locked on the burning house. "I've waited fifty years." She grasped Cameo's hand. "I was the rightful mistress in line for Topazus." Her tone of voice had weakened. Tears streaked her face, dripping large splotches onto the blue gown smudged with dirt. "Your father and I were to marry. We had the blessing of your grandparents."

Cameo nodded slowly. "You told me how Grandmother Lela would let you wear the ring."

Rita stretched the fingers of her gloved right hand upward. The fake ring glistened. Rita's face contorted into a pained expression. "They gave Morgan an ultimatum. Marry Katherine, lose the house. He made the wrong choice. Don't you see? This should have never happened."

Cameo recoiled. "My grandparents gave my father an ultimatum?"

Rita continued to stare at the flames and nodded. Slowly, she closed her fingers into a fist and using her left hand, pressed on top of the ring until her neck tendons bulged. "Morgan gave Topazus over to the likes of Berdanier. He cared that little. He didn't deserve ownership. Lela said so." Holding her gripped hands in front of her, Rita began twisting her wrists in rhythm with the savage twirling flames.

Body language was the tool of a lawman. Rita's hands unmasked her despair.

"Move back!" A fireman yelled.

Boom!

A support beam cracked, then crashed in an

explosive flash of vicious fury.

Rita continued, trance-like, "Lela let me wear the ring. She told me it would be mine one day." Her clasped hands sprung loose. She seized the fake ring, yanked it off and whirled around. "But James took it." Like the strike of a coiled rattlesnake, she thrust her accusation and the ring at James. He flinched as the ring drilled into his chest.

You told me that Alfred Berdanier was going to take the topaz ring, and I would go to jail for fraud. You said I had to stop him." Her eyes narrowed into slits.

Then just as quickly as she lashed out at James, Rita relaxed. With a sigh of resignation, she said, "I know Martha Lee. She would never have done what she did if Daniel hadn't told her to." She wiped the mucous from her nose.

Cameo looked at Robert then Officer Kelley, a tear trailed her flushed cheek. She turned back to the woman sitting next to her. "Rita, did James tell Martha Lee to shoot Alfred Berdanier?"

James lunged forward. "Cameo." His voice a seething whisper. "What are you doing?"

Eyes fixed on James; Rita said. "Yes. I knew it the second after I pulled the trigger, but James is my son. James you should never have taken the topaz. I could have protected you if it weren't for Martha Lee."

"Can't you see the woman is mad?" Red splotches crept above the stiff 1800s collar on James' neck. He ran desperate eyes to Robert and then Officer Kelley. "You see that don't you? She's deranged."

Cameo's shoulders slumped. She turned her back on James. "And the apple doesn't fall far from the tree."

CHAPTER NINETEEN

On the stone steps of Crest Manor, Robert's shoes crunched against charred remains from the Topazus fire. Jane, ahead of him, stopped her ascent and turned around.

She looked beyond him down the hill at the burned hulk of Topazus. "Even with its problems, it's a shame the mansion was destroyed."

The sun penetrated the trees and spotlighted the grim results of last night's fire. Could he have handled the situation differently and avoided the destruction? The last time Robert mounted these steps, Katherine had confessed to shooting Berdanier. His gut told him she didn't commit the murder and his instincts urged him to pursue the ring to uncover whoever did.

Rita's confession had led to James' arrest and her being admitted to a mental health facility.

A soot-covered squirrel skittered along the ground. "There's one little fellow that escaped Katherine's sights," Robert said.

Jane giggled and pointed at a cardinal with his head tilted toward gray flaked seeds in his feeder.

Her laughter was uplifting. So far, their goal of a restful time away from the detective agency hadn't happened. At least with the murder solved, maybe some semblance of their Christmas holiday could be salvaged.

Robert rang the doorbell, and Cameo greeted them.

"Welcome to the B & B's replacement breakfast location. Robert why the glum face? Your strategy solved the murder."

"But the fire. I should have been ready for Rita's erratic behavior."

Cameo shook her head. "You can put that worry to rest. According to the fire chief, the likely cause was the power strip in the music room overheating and igniting the drapes. I witnessed the fire jump to the windowsills and wallpaper. The progression was too rapid to do anything but get out. And thankfully, everyone did. Come on. We can talk over breakfast."

Katherine and Dean had set up a buffet on the kitchen island.

"I like to keep things simple. Serve yourselves and have a seat," Katherine said.

Using disposable plates and utensils, everyone helped themselves to grits, scrambled eggs, bacon, and toast. Topazus' fine china and silver were destroyed but Robert silently rejoiced in not having to worry about what fork to use.

"Try my homemade pear preserves," Katherine said, placing a jar on the table. "What I'd like to know, Robert, is how you convinced Officer Kelley to investigate Rita and James instead of me?"

Robert shook his head, "Kelley had a surprising change of heart. When I first talked to him, he had his killer, and he sure wasn't interested in my theories about ashes and the status of the ring."

"When the insurance people questioned me about the ring, I suspected Berdanier faked the theft for the insurance money, not Rita or James," Cameo said. "What put you on to the ring being in Rita's possession?"

"Jane's keen eye. Fill them in." He'd caught her with a mouth full.

She grabbed her napkin and dabbed at her mouth and jumped into the conversation. Not only was she insightful, she was a good sport.

"Two things. The ring Rita wore on the YouTube video Cameo shared looked authentic and was filmed after the insurance theft claim."

Cameo made a puzzled frown but kept quiet.

"Second, after the mother-daughter tea, I saw Rita in the dressing room, chattering as Martha Lee, while she admired the ring in the light from the window. The brilliance that flashed from that ring screamed genuine topaz."

Dean huffed. "That doesn't surprise me. She always had a fetish about that ring."

"I had seen the original when I visited here years ago," Jane said. "Rita startled when she saw me enter the costume room and rolled the ring up in her gloves. I found it odd that she covered it up."

"Another mystery was the computer drive that disappeared while we were in the library," Robert said.

Katherine returned from the kitchen with the coffee pot. "What computer drive?"

Cameo took the coffee pot and freshened cups around the table. "We were viewing a drive from Berdanier's office in the library. The lights went out, and when they came back on the drive was gone."

Katherine waved a hand. "I've always said there was something strange about that house."

"Not just the house but the people in it." Robert braced himself. Cameo hadn't heard this part. "I found the drive by accident a couple of days later hidden in a secret drawer in the library mantle."

"Secret drawer?" Cameo plunked the coffee carafe on the table. Fortunately, it was empty, or Robert might have had hot brew running down his back. "Why am I just hearing about this?"

Robert lifted his hands. "Because everyone involved with Topazus had to be considered a suspect. Jane downloaded the files from the drive, and I sent it off to be fingerprinted."

"Ah, that explains Jane's wanting those cups for her snowflake project." Cameo put a fist to her hip. "You were gathering our fingerprints. *All* our prints. And *I* hired you." Her steely eyes could best be described as glaring. "So, what did you find out?"

"The drive had your thumbprint."

"Oh, great." Her exasperation with him melded into disgust, and she sank to her chair.

Robert kept his grin inside. "Your print on the drive wasn't surprising. You pushed the drive in the port on the computer, and the person who removed it could grasp the sides, not disturbing your print."

"So, who took it?"

"James," Jane said. "He tipped his hand when he mentioned my Aunt Bessie Lawrence from Florence.

The only time I made that remark was when Robert and I were alone in the library the night the lights went out. James had to have been listening from the hidden space behind the wall."

Cameo leaned forward. "Austins from Boston. That's what the rhyming stuff was about? But why hide the drive? James and I both saw the information on Berdanier's computer when it was released."

"At the time, James didn't know what was on the drive," Robert said. "James took the files from the briefcase before he reported finding Berdanier's body too. Since Berdanier had the Topazus ring on his agenda, James needed time to retrieve the ring and sell it. His mother would have never parted with it willingly. He believed Berdanier knew his mother had made a fraudulent theft report."

"But still—"

The doorbell rang, interrupting Katherine.

Cameo went to the door and returned with SLED Agent Kelley.

"Sorry to interrupt folks," Kelley said.

"Have a seat and eat breakfast with us," Katherine said. "That is if you aren't planning to haul me off to jail."

He offered a forlorn twist of his mouth. "I deserve the admonition and thank you for the offer. I've eaten breakfast, but I'll take coffee."

"I'll get it, Mom."

Cameo took the empty pot and went to the kitchen.

"I felt that I owed you an update." Officer Kelley's cockiness had disappeared. "Our office had the jeweler, John Oliver, under surveillance for dealing in stolen property. When you dropped his name," he nodded toward Robert, "I thought it best not to be in cross purposes."

Robert's estimation of Kelley took an uptick.

"After Rita accused her son of taking the ring, we obtained a search warrant for the jewelry store. We found the ring."

That revelation delivered shocked expressions around the table; Robert included.

"However," he tugged at his ear, "he had already cut the gem into five smaller stones and removed the diamonds from the original setting."

Cameo returned to the table and handed a fresh-brewed cup of coffee to Officer Kelley. "To think we were so close to getting it back."

"We've charged Oliver with dealing in stolen property. He paid James twenty thousand dollars for the ring and stood to gain a lot more selling the remade jewelry."

"The day the roof at the mansion was inspected, James came and left in a big hurry. That could be when he took the ring," Jane said. "The roofer mentioned seeing James on the casino ship at Myrtle Beach."

Officer Kelley shrugged at the plausibility. "James told Oliver he was in a tight spot and had to pay off a debt."

Cameo said, "Gambling debt, I imagine. James had asked me for a loan until he could access an investment account, and then a few days ago I saw the mantle clock from Topazus in his car. He said his mother was concerned it might be too valuable to leave unguarded on the mantle and wanted him to have it appraised." Cameo shook her head. "I should have picked up on the clues. Especially when he invited me to dinner on the offshore gambling ship and mentioned he was a member of the Platinum Club."

"All telltale signs." Robert tapped the table. "Borrowing money, lying, taking items to sell or pawning them are all indicators of a gambling problem." He turned to Officer Kelley. "Myrtle Beach Pawn, listed on Berdanier's computer drive, is likely to be significant."

Kelley made eye contact with Robert that acknowledged him as a fellow lawman instead of an adversary. "You're right. Rita ranted about missing items. We'll check into it."

Turning to Katherine, Kelley said, "I admit, I believed I had an open and shut case when I arrested you. Then when Investigator Grey showed up talking about grilled steak ashes, a stolen ring that wasn't stolen, and a missing computer drive that had been hidden, I knew he was wasting my time."

"That was evident when I left your office, what changed your mind?"

"Her." Kelley pointed and all eyes followed the direction he signaled which rested on Jane. She turned a lovely shade of pink. "Ms. Carson came back in the office after you left and shamed me into thinking there might be another explanation in the case."

"What did you say?" Robert asked.

She pressed her hands to her flushed cheeks. "I simply repeated what you taught me. Everyone is a suspect until they are not a suspect."

Cameo slumped in her seat. "Even the person paying them to investigate."

~

After Officer Kelley left and breakfast items were

cleared and washed, everyone gathered in the great room.

Dean sat directly in front of Robert. "Help me understand the significance of the ashes you gathered."

Explaining the if-then way his mind operated to solve a crime might not be easy to put into words. Robert pressed his lips together. Where to begin? He'd start with the most important clue. "In order to access to the murder weapon, the murderer would have had to walk through the ashes spilled around the grill. Forensics said those ashes matched the soot that wound up on my shoes. If I didn't walk in those ashes, then it became a matter of connecting the dots to find the murderer."

Katherine's brows pressed together. "Then you knew Rita shot Berdanier?"

"To be honest, I still didn't know until after the fire. James clearly recognized that his mother could take on a separate distinct personality by the way he spoke to her."

"Like a split personality?" Dean asked.

Cameo chimed in. "I represented the parent of a child with the disorder due to emotional trauma in a school board case. Under pressure, the student slipped into a separate identity. She was granted special accommodations during testing and assistance from a school psychologist."

"As a teacher, I've dealt with students who require special plans," Jane said. "Hopefully, Rita receives the help she needs."

"I keep seeing Rita sitting next to me," Cameo gave a slow shake of her head, "talking about the awful thing Martha Lee had to do."

Dean frowned. "I believe Rita's trauma centered around that blasted ring. She was obsessed with the idea that she was the rightful owner. I suspected James had financial problems, but never that he'd manipulate his mother to ki…" He choked on the word.

Robert said. "People who would never consider such an act, when pushed into a corner, see murder as their only way out. James was desperate for money and must have been convinced Berdanier was ready to turn in him and his mother for fraud."

"But I'm still trying to envision exactly what happened," Katherine said.

"Piecing together what we know, here's what I believe," Robert said. "Rita drove cart number one with James to Crest Manor. James had heard at the luncheon where to find the .22 rifle and knew his mother was an excellent marksman. He spoke to her Martha Lee identity and sent her to retrieve the rifle. She stepped in the ashes which got on the cart's pedals going to and from the shooting. Jane also spotted proof." He nodded for her to share.

"I saw one of the prepared craft pinecones at the shooting site. The cones were in a box on cart one and tipped over when Robert drove it, so apparently it tipped over at the shooting site too, leaving a cone behind."

Robert nodded, chuckling. "A kindergarten teacher spotted a clue that the crime scene specialists missed— me too for that matter."

"Wow. I'm pleased my craft work and Jane's sharp eyes helped solve the case," Katherine said. "How did the garden shoes get involved?"

"After the ladies' tea on Saturday, I met Jane by

the service porch and noticed the ash-coated shoes. It didn't mean anything to me until later when I realized ashes could be a factor."

"Rita's shoes were hurting her feet. She must have slipped on the clogs when she went to the manor with James." Jane said.

Katherine snapped her fingers. "I get it. The ashes on Robert's shoes came from the garden shoes that transferred ashes to the pedals on the cart proven to be at the site where the shot was fired."

"And since you and Dean used the cart from the manor, which was ash free, it should have removed you from suspicion," Cameo said and cut her eyes to both Katherine and Dean. "Even so, you two ran around confessing to the crime."

Dean grasped his knees. "I couldn't stand by and have Katherine accused of murder when I knew she didn't do it."

"Why did you suddenly confess to the murder?" Cameo asked her mother.

She glanced at Cameo, then looked down. "I was afraid you did it."

Cameo's jaw went slack. "Did everyone suspect me?" She glanced at Robert. "Why would I kill Berdanier?"

Katherine's eyes glistened. "He brought up ... Sandra Cathey. Dragging up the accident could have ruined your career."

"Mom, I'd hate to have that come up too, but I would never—"

"I thought if I confessed, the investigation would end."

Cameo briefly closed her eyes and puffed out a

quiet exhale. She took her mother's hand. "I appreciate that you were willing to sacrifice for me. But you should have known Berdanier loved to wield his weight and rattle cages for the shock appeal. I've long since made my peace with the Catheys."

Katherine sniffed. "You're right. I should have known."

"I'm still curious about the house and trying to cover up the deteriorating condition." Jane said. "For what purpose?"

"Financial is my guess," Katherine said pulling a tissue from her pocket and blowing her nose. "Topazus was a big plus for Rita's catering business. She had an unhealthy attachment to that house and refused to see any of the problems."

Dean said, "Rita made no secret to me after we married that she believed she was the rightful heir to the house, the ring, and the position of mistress."

"And I preferred her taking the role," Katherine said. "Lela and Stanford Clark made me feel unwelcome because I was not the chosen one for their son. It may seem strange, but the house rejected me too. It literally made me sick with an upset stomach to go there. In recent years, I had trouble with headaches, watering eyes and sneezing if I was there any length of time."

"That was probably due to the mold prevalent in the hidden spaces," Jane said.

"Some of those spots were news to me," Cameo said. "Although when I heard about Rita and the jewelry box, I have a fuzzy memory of Grandmother showing me a drawer inside." Cameo threw up her hands. "But it's gone now, along with the house.

Grandmother Clark wouldn't like to hear me say this, but the house burning to the ground is a blessing in disguise."

"Amen to that," Katherine said. "Fire took care of the roof, electrical problems, mold, rats and the debate to renovate or tear down."

Jane raised her hand like a student in her classroom. "I can attest to the fire getting rid of the rat problem. Two of those critters ran over Robert and me getting out of there."

Cameo laughed. "Mary Sue said when a giant rat ran through the kitchen and out the back door, she decided it was time to leave too. She shared with me last night that she'd been offered her old job back at the Calhoun's."

"Good," Jane said. "Maybe she can attend college full-time again. She was upset that Berdanier caused her to lose her job. He claimed Calhoun would be hurt politically with her living at his house but she doubted that was the real concern."

She stopped and looked at Robert, seeking an okay to tell what Mary Sue had said. He waved at her to continue. "Mary Sue thought Berdanier's real concern was her overhearing plans to have environmental rules changed in order to clear the way for mineral exploration."

Cameo nodded. "I found out that Berdanier was pushing legislation that would make it easier for a section of the estate to be tested for mineral content. I'll look at what he was pursuing, but not before I square things with Micah."

"Micah called me this morning," Robert said. "He had wanted to tell me something before the electrical accident and remembered what it was."

"And?" Cameo asked.

"At the bonfire he felt pressed to relate a Freedman family tradition that property ownership on Topazus was documented and not just verbal." Robert looked at Jane. "He wanted to ask that I try to find the proof but held back."

"And you did find proof. I'll see to it that the deed Jane found is filed." Cameo pushed out of her chair. "However, we have a more pressing problem."

Katherine sighed heavily, dropping her hands in her lap with a smack. "For heaven's sakes, what now?"

"The Christmas Eve reenactment."

CHAPTER TWENTY

Jane, playing the role of Sarah, lifted the hoop rib under her skirt slightly and perched on the edge of the pew in the Topazus Chapel. Beside her were Cameo in the role of Martha Lee Clark and Robert as Daniel Clark.

Katherine, who said the only role she cared to play was Cameo's present-day mother, sat with Dean on the opposite end of the pew. Sitting with his family in front of them was Micah, dressed in a simple cotton shirt and knee-length trousers of the 1800s. As the loyal thread connecting the Topazus estate from its origins to the present, Cameo had begun legal procedures for deeding property to him.

Jane sensed a variety of emotions inside the little church. Some visitors were there out of curiosity because of the latest drama. Others were faithful participants who saw the Christmas Eve celebration as a treasured family tradition. This latter group was the reason Cameo and her mother decided to not cancel the church service. Rev. Earnest Rivers, Director of Low Country Bible College, agreed to conduct the candlelight ceremony.

To accommodate the crowd, audio speakers were set up for the overflow.

Glancing about the tiny church, Jane searched for Adam. He had said he'd try to come. She bit at her lower lip, hoping his health wouldn't interfere. Her phone tucked in her waistband vibrated. Micah? She peeked at the screen. Evan, her assistant principal at the elementary school.

Just a reminder. I'm still holding that January teaching position open. You don't want to lose your benefits and I can't guarantee an opening if you wait until the fall. Merry Christmas, Evan.

Really? On Christmas Eve? If nothing else, he was persistent.

Robert leaned over to her and spoke softly. "Anything important?"

"Evan Armstrong, reminding me that time is running out on the teaching job he's holding for me," she whispered.

"And?"

"And I'm on leave until next school year. I don't know if you'll continue to need me but with Adam and this kidney thing—"

"I do need you as long as I can have you."

Warmth flooded through her. Jane averted her head. She was reading way too much into that sentence.

Robert reached for a hymnal, then began flipping pages.

She tucked her phone away. She had turned down the offer for the teaching job to begin in January, but reasons to reconsider tumbled in her head. Kindergarten job openings were sometimes scarce. There were retirement benefits and health insurance to consider. The insurance would be important if she became a kidney donor. But if she had surgery to help her brother, she'd be out of school which would be unfair to students. If she stayed with the agency, being out with surgery would be unfair to Robert.

Robert's shoulder brushed against hers. He looked handsome in his waistcoat and high-necked collar with the ascot. He had been her rock, helping her sort out her emotions and resentment toward her brother. Robert had told Jane that she was a help to him in his agency. It would be thankless to abandon him for her teaching job. Or was now a good time to leave at the close of this case and the end of their adventurous vacation?

Rev. Rivers began the service with everyone singing *Joy to the World*. They stood and Robert stuck a hymnal in front of her. Then as the song came to an end, he turned to her and grinned as he sang the last "and wonders of his love" directly to her. The endearment took her breath away. The corset probably contributed. She smiled back at him. He held her elbow, helping her sit and arrange her skirt.

"On my way here," Reverend Rivers began, "I noticed the seemingly dead trees. But I know those trees will surprise us come spring. The Topazus home tragically burned to the ground. All seems dead and bleak, but just as new growth springs up after the dark days of winter so will the Topazus legacy of faith and forgiveness continue."

His lesson steamrolled Jane's heart as she internalized the forgiveness she felt for her own brother. Yet she longed for Adam to forgive her.

A jab to her ribs made Jane jump.

"Are you coming? It's showtime."

"Sorry." She'd missed their cue. Robert took her hand and helped her navigate the pew. Cameo and Micah followed.

The pastor narrated. "At the close of the Christmas Eve service in 1865, Martha Lee Clark with her daughter, Sarah and son Daniel, who had served as a Union soldier, filed from the church at midnight. The prayer on their heart was the safe return of Davis, whose convictions had led him to take a stand with the Confederacy. Following behind them was Joe Clark Freedman, a slave freed before the Civil War by Topazus plantation owner, Morgan Danford Clark. Joe had chosen to remain and help keep the estate running."

Outside, Jane took her designated place on the edge of the gravel drive near the famous Reconciliation Cedar Tree. The congregation, each holding a candle, became spectators.

"Be sure I don't miss my cue this time," she whispered to Robert.

"Rule number six. I've got your back." His smile and light touch to her waist warmed her heart. He had proven to be a good backup, supporting her decision to be tested as a donor for Adam. Jane scanned the crowd again, hoping to glimpse of her brother. Her pulse surged. There was Bethany and the boys, but ... no Adam. Was he not well enough to come? She sent Bethany a quick smile.

When all were assembled, Cameo stepped up to deliver her lines as Martha Lee. What must be running through her mind, taking the role that Rita had played for so long? She had admitted to emotional hurt but accepted the part. "I'll just apply what lawyering has taught me. Never let personal feelings get in the way of delivering what the jury needs to hear."

She spoke, and her diction and poise were perfection. "Pastor, Sarah, Daniel, Joe and friends I am so grateful that you are with me at this Christmas Eve candlelight service. We can all be thankful the war has ended. I pray for each of you a blessed Christmas. As families reunite, please pray with me that my son Davis, still missing after this dreadful war, will find his way home."

On cue, Reverend Rivers lit his candle and lit the person's next to him. "Peace be with you, pass the light."

Each person repeated the phrase and the ceremonial lighting spread pools of light throughout the group, illuminating each face. The moment surreal. When the last candle was lit, Micah's son, Casey, began ringing the church bell, announcing Christmas Day. On the twelfth strike, Micah, playing the part of his ancestor, shouted, "Look! Someone is coming!"

Cameo, Jane and Robert turned toward the dirt road as they had rehearsed. Emerging out of the shadows formed by the trees penetrated by bits of moonlight, came a figure moving slowly. As the form drew closer, Jane could see the man's torn pants, his knees exposed. Strips of cloth were tied around his feet. He limped and he wore a scruffy beard. His reaching the giant cedar tree, was Jane's signal.

"Davis!" she shouted and ran to him, grabbing him in a hug. "You're alive!"

"I hope so, Sis."

"What?" Jane pulled back and stared at the man underneath the beard. "Adam?"

His cheeks stretched his mouth so wide light shone on his teeth.

"You came." She grabbed him, hugging harder, and took in the warmth of her brother's arms.

More hugs followed as scripted and Robert delivered his line in a powerful voice, "I've prayed every day you'd make it home."

When Cameo said, "Praise God, we are a family again," the preacher began singing. "Silent night, holy night ..." and soft voices blended as one in song.

Leaning into her brother's shoulder and with the soft press of Robert's hand to her back, the words arose past leafless, dormant trees of winter into a starlit night filled with hope.

Dear Reader,

I hope you enjoyed this book that was written in large part during the coronavirus pandemic. It has been interesting to hear people share in various forms of media their reactions to the recommendation to stay-at-home. Many are discovering anew the art of conversation and reading books--things they didn't seem to have time for before. On the other hand, some share that pet peeves and frustrations more readily surface and irritate.

When the characters in *Winter Deception* came together, discoveries were made too. I've heard the expression, "if these walls could talk, what would they say?" So, I pondered the question for Topazus. What might happen if the antebellum manor divulged its secrets? It turned out that as Topazus' problems were revealed so were the character's issues of bitterness, greed and deception.

In case the signature chicken entrée served at the luncheon in the opener charged up your taste buds, I experimented with a recipe and included it for you. Join me at my website where I am investigating foods authors use in their novels and you'll find more recipes and book information. I enjoy hearing from readers. Drop me a note under "contact me" at www.sallyjopitts.com, and I invite you to join me in Robert and Jane's next Seasons of Mystery case coming in the spring.

Topazus **CRANBERRY ORANGE CHICKEN**

Ingredients:
4-5 chicken thighs or breasts
½ c. whole cranberries (plus extra for garnish)
1 Tbsp. honey
1 Tbsp. olive oil

Marinade:
¼ c. cranberries
1 Tbsp. brown sugar
2 Tbsp. olive oil
2 Tbsp. honey
1 Tbsp. balsamic vinegar
2 cloves garlic, minced
1 Tbsp. orange zest (plus extra for garnish)
¼ c. tart cherry juice
¼ tsp. salt
1/8 tsp. black pepper

Instructions:

Prepare marinade:
Blend marinade ingredients in a food processor until smooth. Add chicken to large Ziplock bag. Pour marinade over chicken and marinate for one hour or overnight. Add chicken to a roasting pan. Pour marinade over. Spread ½ c. whole cranberries evenly over chicken. Bake at 375 for 30 minutes. Mix 1 Tbsp.

honey and 1 Tbsp. olive oil, brush on chicken. Broil 2-3 minutes to lightly brown. Discard marinade. Serve chicken garnished with additional cranberries and orange zest.

About the author:

Sally Jo Pitts brings a career as a private investigator, high school guidance counselor and teacher of family and consumer sciences to the fiction page. Tapping into her real-world experiences, she writes what she likes to read—faith-based stories, steeped in the mysteries of life's relationships. She is author of *Autumn Vindication*, book #1 in the Seasons of Mystery Series. You can connect with her at www.sallyjopitts.com.